Crave

www.chellebliss.com

CHELLE BLISS
USA TODAY BESTSELLING AUTHOR

COPYRIGHT

Published by Chelle Bliss on 5.2.24 & 10.31.24
Edited by Silently Correcting Your Grammar
Proofread by Shelley Charlton
Cover Design © Chelle Bliss
Formatting by Chelle Bliss

thank you for buying the print edition

Download the eBook version for FREE!

Scan the QR code below, add the eBook to your cart, and the 100% discount will be shown at checkout.

the eBook will be instantly delivered to your email via Bookfunnel

CHAPTER 1
TATE

"HAPPY BIRTHDAY, SWEETHEART," Dad says as I lean over my birthday cake, trying not to catch my hair on fire.

"Make a wish," my grandmother says from across the table.

Every year, I wish for the impossible. Not surprisingly, it's never granted. This year, I decided I'd wish for something else, but it may be just as impossible as my usual dream.

I close my eyes and think of what my perfect life would look like. I want what my grandmother has...a large family of my own someday. I inhale a big breath, needing as much air as possible to blow out the ridiculous number of candles my stepmother Tilly placed on the cake.

"What did you wish for?" my youngest brother Mason asks me as soon as I blow out the candles.

"You never tell a wish," I say to him as I do every year when he asks me the same question.

"Someday you'll slip up." He smiles at me. "And when you do, I'll be here for it."

"I never make mistakes," I tease him with a wink.

My other brother, Brax, snorts from Mason's other side. "I have one word...Rowdy."

I roll my eyes, hating that I'll always be reminded of the biggest mistake of my life. If I could go back in time and make it so I never met him, I'd do it in a heartbeat.

Rowdy was a very long phase in my life. We were never serious, but the man took up enough of my time to make it damn near impossible for me to meet anyone else. I was all about fun back then, and if there was a perfect word to describe Rowdy, it would be "fun." The second would be "womanizer," but in my early twenties, I didn't want to be tied down either.

What started as fun turned into something entirely different, and my casual relationship with Rowdy almost ended my life.

"Rowdy was a learning experience, not a mistake," I tell Brax.

I have to think of him that way, because a mistake should only happen once, not many times spanning years. When everything with Rowdy finally ended, I knew what I wanted, and it didn't include being unimportant in my partner's life.

I wanted it all. I wanted what my father had with my mother before she died and with Tilly when he finally remarried. I wanted a man who would look out for me, love me, and be fierce in his loyalty.

"He was also a dick," Brax adds.

Tilly slides a piece of cake in front of me, thankfully

interrupting our conversation. "The first piece for the birthday girl."

Tilly is the best kind of human. She is sweet, kind, and caring, with a hint of sass that sometimes has me doubling over in laughter. I couldn't have picked a better step-mother than her. It didn't hurt that she owned a cupcake shop when I was little. What girl doesn't want an unlimited supply of sweets at her disposal?

"Thanks, Ma." I smile up at her as I take the plate and move it closer. "It looks delicious. You outdid yourself."

Tilly places her hand on my shoulder and squeezes. "Only the best for you, sweetheart."

"I want a big piece, Ma," Mason tells her. "A corner with tons of frosting. I'm a growing boy."

She stares at Mason and shakes her head. "First, you're not a boy, and you haven't grown an inch in years. But I'll still get you a big piece because you're the only one who has a bottomless pit of a stomach for frosting."

"I was born with a sweet tooth," he says unapologetically. It's amazing how few cavities Mason has with the amount of sugar he ingests every day.

"If only you were as sweet as the food you ate," Zoey, my cousin, teases Mason from across the table. "Instead of being the giant asshole you really are."

"I'm an angel," Mason replies, lifting his hands above his head to adjust his invisible halo.

Nino slides into the chair next to Zoey and glances around at us. "What'd I miss?"

"Mason's an angel," Brax answers.

"An angel?" Nino asks in disbelief. "I don't remember Carla using that word to describe him."

"Carla's just bitter that I broke up with her."

"She was mint, Mas. You're an idiot for ending that relationship."

"I'm too young to be tied down," my brother says as he digs into his cake like he hasn't eaten in a decade.

He sounds like me at his age. I thought I had all the time in the world and didn't want to miss a moment of fun. But time passed quickly, and now I'm thirty, with nothing to show for it except a few memories.

"Are we going out after this?" Zoey asks, smoothing back her long hair.

"That's the plan. I got us on a list for the new club downtown," Brax replies, always having connections everywhere.

"Nice," Nino whispers. "I heard it's amazing."

"Can I tap out?" I ask, not feeling like partying tonight.

"What?" Brax asks. "We're going to celebrate your birthday, goofball. You have to go."

"You'll have fun without me."

"Come on, cousin. I even had it cleared so we can bring in the younger ones," Nino says.

Great. Underage kids in a nightclub. Sounds like the perfect way to spend the night of my birthday.

"I have my period, and my cramps are horrible." It's a dirty lie, but I know any mention of girl things like cramps or, God forbid, a period, and all the males will immediately back off.

"That sucks," Zoey says, frowning in understanding. "I hate when that happens."

"I'd rather go home and sit with my heating pad and curl up with a good book."

"Man," Mason mutters as he shakes his head. "Thirty really is the turning point to old age."

I punch his arm, loving that he winces. "You're a jerk."

"We've established that." He chuckles as he rubs his arm, where I hope he'll have a small bruise. "But at least I'm a young and fun jerk."

"We can all hang out at your place," Amelia finally says, entering the conversation. She's the shyest one of us all and likes to follow along instead of lead. I don't blame her either. This bunch can be a bit much sometimes.

My stomach drops at the thought of some of the messiest humans I've ever known being at my place. One at a time, I can deal with, but in a group…no way. It would take me a week to clean up in their wake. "No. No. Go downtown and have fun. I insist."

"You're coming out for my birthday, sis," Brax says. "No excuses next time."

"You're on, brother."

Crisis averted.

CHAPTER 2
TATE

MY EYES STOP on the photo of my family from twenty-five years ago that has been hanging behind the bar since the day it was taken.

My mother was close to my age but somehow looked younger than I do now. Her face was filled with so much happiness, without a clue of what was to come.

There is a twinge in my chest, the same ache I always feel when I think about the hole that was left behind by her death.

Time isn't consistent when it comes to grief either. Somehow it feels like yesterday and a long time ago, all at the same time.

"Tate, you've got to handle this," Alyssa, my best friend since we were little kids, says.

She moved away years ago, but she's come for a visit and wanted to help at the bar so my brother Brax could have a night off.

I blink away my sadness and shake my head. "Handle what?"

As I turn toward Alyssa, she dips her head toward the barstools. "Them."

I let out a loud breath, readying myself for whatever nonsense I am about to turn around to see. In my lifetime, I've seen some crazy things at the Hook and Hustle, my family's bar on the Southside of Chicago.

But when I spin, I'm quickly taken aback. There are two girls seated at the bar, looking entirely out of place.

The oldest is maybe fifteen with straight, long brown hair and the biggest brown eyes I'd ever seen. The younger one looks entirely different, with red hair pulled back in a braid, light green eyes, and freckles.

"Jesus," I mutter, wondering how they wandered in here and took a seat in the short time I had my back turned.

"My thoughts exactly," Alyssa whispers before sauntering away with a pitcher of beer, leaving me to deal with them.

"Hey, girls," I say softly, taking a step forward. "You're a little young to be in here. Is your dad or mom here?" I look around the bar, but I see no new faces these two could belong to.

"No," the oldest girl says without giving any more information.

Teenage girls are the worst. So full of attitude and anger, mostly caused by hormones, but amplified by the stupidity of teenage boys.

The youngest pulls on the sleeve of the older girl. "Sissy, I want a Shirley Temple," the little girl whispers.

I smile at the mention of an old favorite. Every little girl has their Shirley Temple phase, and mine was longer than most because it was a drink my mother always made me and my family owned a bar. I thought I looked cool drinking one, and it didn't hurt that it tasted good too.

"We'll take two Shirley Temples," the older girl says, looking like she isn't about to leave, even though they are both too young to be in here.

I take a few steps forward and lean over the bar in front of them. "You two can't be here by yourselves. Where's your mom or dad?"

The older one's face immediately sours. "Our mom moved to Oregon, and I don't know where our dad is."

"He's at work," the younger one says, earning herself a glare from her sister.

My heart immediately hurt for the girls. I couldn't imagine my mother moving across the country, leaving us behind by choice.

What kind of woman leaves her kids behind?

An awful one.

"Maybe we can call him," I say and start to reach under the bar for my phone.

"No," the older girl snaps. "He's not allowed to receive calls at work. I'm in charge."

"Really?" My gaze dips to the little girl, who can't seem to look me in the eyes anymore, alerting me to the fact that the older one is lying.

"Can we please get two Shirley Temples, and then we'll go?" the older one asks, fidgeting on the stool.

In that moment, I think about my dad and what he'd do if he were here instead of me. He'd give the girls what they wanted and face the consequences later.

"How about we make a deal? You tell me if your dad knows where you are, and your names, and I'll make you two Shirley Temples on the house."

The older one's gaze dips to her little sister. "Fine," she sighs, clearly annoyed. "I'm Maddox, and this is Hazel."

Hazel gives me a giant smile as her upper body sways, her legs no doubt swinging around under the bar out of nervousness. "We call her Maddy, and they call me Haze."

"Zip it," Maddox tells her sister, deflating the little girl just a bit. "And yes, he knows where we are."

"He does?" Hazel asks as she peers up at her sister with those big green eyes.

"Yep," she snaps a little too quickly, letting me know that her answer is a lie.

"Do I know your dad?" I ask, hoping to get more information, because something about this doesn't sit right with me.

Maddox shrugs. "We're new around here."

That is obvious. I know almost every single person in the neighborhood, and I've never seen the two girls before now.

That's how it is around here. We live in a big city, but the neighborhood is tight. Most of the residents have been here for decades, but there are more new faces now that some of the older folks have started to die off.

"We used to live downtown, but now we live down the street," Hazel says, sounding much older than she is. "Dad couldn't afford to keep the loft for long after Mom left."

"Mom left us four years ago, Hazel. That's not why. This is closer to his work, and he wanted us to grow up in a house with a yard." Maddox gags. "I hate it."

"I like the yard," Hazel tells Maddox, pulling at the tip of her long braid that's draped over her shoulder. "I want a swing."

I start to make the Shirley Temples, going as slowly as I

can, hoping to buy some time for either their father to show up or someone to come looking for them. "Do you babysit your sister often when your dad is at work?"

"Sometimes," Maddox replies.

Hazel shakes her head as she twists her body on the stool, unable to sit still with all her youthful energy. "Granny's watching us."

"She is?" I ask, peering around the bar and not seeing a grandma anywhere. Besides me, Maddox, Hazel, and Alyssa, there are only a few other females in the bar, and I know them all.

"She fell asleep," Hazel informs me, earning herself a jab in the ribs from Maddox's elbow.

I set their drinks in front of them and decide to push for more information. "Does she know you're here?"

"Yeah."

"She does?" Hazel asks Maddox.

"Fine." Maddox's shoulders sag forward. "We'll be home before she wakes up."

"Oh boy," I mutter, shaking my head.

If I'd snuck out of my grandma's place while she was napping at their age, I would've got my ass chewed out by her first and my dad later.

"They're Cheryl's grandkids," Marvin, a lifelong regular, says from the other end of the bar. The only time he moves from his stool is to use the bathroom. I swear the cushion is permanently crushed in the form of his bony ass. "I remember her talking about the girls last time I saw her."

Cheryl isn't a drinker. When she does come into the Hook and Hustle, it is for a bite to eat and some company. She's always been sweet to me, and I've never seen her be mean to a soul. There isn't a doubt in my mind that the moment she opens her eyes and realizes the two girls are gone, she'll panic.

"They're Wylder's kids," Marvin explains like I have a single clue who Wylder is.

"Wylder?" Alyssa asks as she passes by Marvin. "Who is he?"

"He's Wylder," Marvin says behind the rim of his beer glass.

"Well, okay," Alyssa replies, shrugging at me when our eyes meet. "Thanks for the explanation, Marv."

"Drink up, ladies, and then I'm taking you back to Cheryl's house."

"We know how to get back," Maddox says as she plucks the cherry from her glass with her clear-coated fingernails.

"Baby girl, I don't care if you know the way or not, I'm walking you back to know you're safe, and in case Cheryl is losing her shit."

Hazel gasps as her eyes become as big as saucers. "Granny said that's a bad word."

"Fuck," I grumble under my breath.

"I heard that," Hazel whispers before she busies herself with her Shirley Temple. "Too bad the swear jar isn't here."

"Way to go." Alyssa pats me on the back, chuckling. "You've always had a potty mouth and an inability to filter."

Maddox finally cracks a smile around the red straw in her drink.

"You know I'm horrible at watching my language, Alyssa. I blame growing up in this bar for it, too."

"You grew up here?" Hazel asks, glancing around the old place. "Where did you sleep?"

Maddox groans and rolls her eyes. "She didn't mean she grew up in the bar, Haze."

"I didn't sleep here. My family owns the bar. I was probably younger than you when I started spending more time here."

"You own this?" Maddox asks and sits a little straighter.

I nod. "My entire family does."

"So, you do this every day?"

"No. I help my stepmom out at the bakery next door sometimes, and I own Inked Southside across the street."

Maddox turns around and stares out the windows. "The tattoo place?"

"Yep."

She turns back to face me, and suddenly, her iciness has disappeared. "That's so cool."

And for a moment, my iciness cools with the hormonal teenage girl who probably enjoys giving her father more than his fair share of trouble. "Now, you have three minutes to finish up, and then we're heading to your granny's place. You've been gone long enough."

"It's not like anyone cares," Maddox mumbles under her breath as she lifts the glass of pink liquid to her lips.

I head down the bar to where Alyssa is talking to Marvin, catching up on all the neighborhood gossip she's missed in the year since her last visit back to the Southside. "Teenagers," Alyssa says to me when I'm out of earshot of the girls. "They're the best birth control ever."

"That's no lie, bestie. They're impossible," I tell her.

"Were we that bad at that age?" she asks me.

Marvin clears his throat and mutters, "One hundred percent."

"You remember us back then?" I ask him, always shocked at how many people in the bar I've known basically my entire life.

"You two were big-time troublemakers. I don't know how your parents survived." He deflates as soon as the words leave his mouth. "I'm sorry, Tate. I didn't mean that how it sounded. God rest your mother's soul."

I move to stand in front of him, resting my hip against the counter, not the least bit upset. "Marvin, I know you weren't talking about my mom. She never got to see me make it to my troublemaker years."

"And when exactly did the troublemaker years end, Tate? Because I'm pretty sure that Rowdy didn't exit the picture that long ago."

I sigh at the mention of his name. The man who almost stole my heart along with my life. He was nothing but trouble, and yet, I couldn't stay away. He wasn't the real problem, but his brothers in his motorcycle club were. If they'd had their way, I wouldn't be standing here now, breathing.

"I left him five years ago. That's a pretty lengthy stretch, and I made a promise to myself as soon as I turned thirty, Alyssa. Didn't I tell you about it?"

She crosses her arms and tilts her head, waiting to hear my bullshit. "No, but I'm really interested in hearing about what I can only assume is stupidity."

I raise my chin because Alyssa knows me better than anyone, and she isn't wrong. I've had my fair share of harebrained ideas, but this isn't one of them. "Since turning thirty, I've sworn off three things."

Her eyebrows rise in surprise. "Oh boy. This should be good."

"No more donuts."

"Good luck with that. Hello. Your stepmom owns a bakery."

"I never said cupcakes were off the table, only donuts." I didn't completely lose my mind when I came up with this bright idea. There's no way I'd ever be able to quit Tilly's cupcakes because they're the best thing I've ever put in my mouth.

"Okay. You're not completely dumb, then. What else?"

I turn around to face her, giving Marvin my back. "No more biker boys."

"I take back everything I said. Maybe you're smarter than you've ever been before."

I smack her shoulder, hating that she's probably right. "The other one is too personal."

"Whisper it to me."

"There's nothing you can't say in front of me," Marvin says, butting into the conversation and always listening to everything. "I won't tell anyone."

Alyssa and I look at each other and burst into laughter because if there's one guy in this bar who's a gossip, it's Marvin.

"I'll fill you in later. I want to get the girls back to Cheryl," I tell Alyssa. "Can you handle things for twenty minutes or so while I'm gone?"

"Take your time. I got you, babe."

"I plan to drop and run," I tell her.

"Good luck. It's Cheryl. She isn't going to let you run."

"I have a feeling she's going to be too upset for company."

CHAPTER 3
TATE

THE SUNSHINE GLINTS off the chrome of the perfectly polished bike as we walk up the driveway to the house.

"Dad's here," Hazel says as we walk by the bike.

"Crap," Maddox mumbles under her breath.

"Please just leave us here," Maddox begs as we climb the steps to her grandmother's two-story brick bungalow with a perfectly manicured front yard.

The door swings open before Hazel's foot reaches the porch, and the entrance is filled by an extremely large man.

Whoa!

And it's not lost on me that the man is also devastatingly handsome. I may have sworn off dating hot bikers, but no one said I couldn't gawk at them and appreciate them for the specimen they are.

The girls stop their movement as soon as their gazes travel up their dad's body to his face.

He doesn't look happy either. One look from him as a

little kid would've sent me running for the hills. But as a woman, I can appreciate the hotness of the man with a scowl so wicked, he could make my panties drop with a single growl against my ear.

"Hey, Daddy," Hazel says, breaking the silence.

Their dad hasn't uttered a word or made a sound since he laid eyes on his girls. I don't think my father could've stayed silent this long if I'd wandered away and he couldn't find me. My family doesn't have the ability to keep our mouths closed, but clearly, this is a skill this man practices—and well.

"Are they back?" Cheryl asks from inside the house, her voice shriller than usual.

"Yup," he barks, moving onto the porch.

I nearly swallow my tongue as the tall drink of water steps into the light of the afternoon sun. His torn jeans, oil-stained shirt, and few days old scruff on his face have my inner biker girl fanatic on high alert.

Don't gawk, Tate. He's a dad.

It doesn't matter how hot the man is. I swore off his type. And he's also in the middle of a crisis, or maybe it is a meltdown.

Cheryl rushes out of the house, knocking into her son as she runs by him. She's on her knees in an instant, pulling the girls into her arms. "Oh my God. I was so worried." She sniffles, squeezing the girls as tightly as she can without hurting them.

"We're sorry, Granny," Maddox tells Cheryl, looking more remorseful than she did the entire time at the bar. It's funny how quickly her teenage attitude disappeared. "Hazel wanted a Shirley Temple, and I thought we'd be back before you got up."

"Bullshit," Wylder grumbles, crossing his arms over his chest. "You know better than that, Maddy."

Oh boy.

Wylder clearly knows the girl likes to pull some shit. I feel an instant kinship to Maddox because I was her many, many years ago.

"Dad," she whines, no doubt pouting at him because it used to work when she was little, but I don't think it's going to get her out of this jam.

"Zip it," he says, sounding very much like Maddy when she said the same thing to Hazel at the bar. "You're too old to be pulling shit like this, Maddy. And to take your sister and put her in danger too is totally irresponsible."

"Don't be so hard on them," Cheryl says to her son as she straightens and wipes at her tearstained cheeks. "You did some boneheaded things when you were their age too. And that's another dollar for the swear jar because of your potty mouth."

My lips twitch at Cheryl's words.

Wylder scrubs a hand across the scruff lining his face. "Can I help you?" he asks me, and any hint of a smile that was forming on my lips dies.

I touch my chest, wishing I had taken a few steps back so I could wander away without being noticed. "I walked them home to make sure they made it safely."

"And you are?" He eyes me suspiciously as if somehow I'm the scarier one of the two of us.

Cheryl smacks her son's chest with the back of her hand. "That's Tate from the Hook and Hustle." Cheryl gives me a faint smile. "Thanks for bringing the girls back. I appreciate it, sweetheart."

"You're welcome, Cheryl. They're good girls."

"I know they are. Thanks, Tate," Cheryl replies.

I don't dare steal a glance at Wylder. I can feel his eyes on me without looking directly at him. He's mad. Not at me, but that doesn't stop me from being a little scared.

"Girls, tell Tate thank you."

"Thanks for the Shirley Temple, Tate," Hazel says, toying with her braid again. "It was the best."

I give the little girl a reassuring smile. "You're welcome."

"Thanks," Maddox says, but there's no sweetness in her tone like there was from Hazel.

I give her a head dip, figuring her statement wasn't sincere and doesn't require a verbal response.

"I appreciate you bringing my kids back." Wylder takes a few steps forward, coming way too close to me. "They're going to be grounded for a long time."

"Dad," they cry in unison.

He lifts a hand, and the girls fall silent. "I don't want to hear it. You nearly gave your grandmother a heart attack."

"Don't listen to him," Cheryl tells the girls, giving them another squeeze. "He'll calm down."

Hazel's sad eyes meet mine, and the heartache I felt for them earlier comes roaring back. Although their situation is different because their mother is alive, I know how they feel—abandoned, lost, and unsure of everything in the future.

"I've got to get back to the bar, Cheryl. Stop in sometime this week and say hi," I say before spinning around on my heel and hustling down the walkway to the sidewalk.

When Cheryl does stop in, I'll ask her about the girls.

Hopefully Wylder will cool off and realize the girls are acting out. I'm sure that will be the case. It's hard to see the problem when you fear for the lives of those you love.

I know my father would've blown a gasket if I'd vanished into thin air without at least leaving a note. Hell, even if I'd left a note, he would've lost his shit. I would've been grounded for weeks for pulling a stunt like that, but he would've eventually come to his senses and realized I was acting out to get attention.

As soon as I get back to the bar, Alyssa comes right for me. "How did it go?"

I draw in a long, shaky breath and plop down in a seat at an empty table. "Cheryl was crying."

"Aw," Alyssa says, sliding into the chair across from me. "She's a sweet old lady. I'm sure she was scared."

"Yeah, she was."

"Was the dad there?"

"Yep." I scrub a hand across my forehead, trying to get the mental image of Wylder out of my mind, but it doesn't work.

"And?"

"He was pissed."

"Well, duh."

"He's grounding them."

"No doubt, but did you recognize him?"

"No. Why would I?"

"Marvin was telling me about him. He grew up in the neighborhood."

"He did?" I scrunch my nose, thinking I knew everyone from around here, but Wylder didn't seem the least bit familiar.

"He's older than us, though, but I don't remember him

even out and about in the neighborhood. He must not have hung around here much because I can't put a face with the name."

"It's a face you wouldn't forget."

Alyssa perks up, straightens her back, and leans closer to me. "Do tell."

"He's hot."

"How hot?"

"He's the type of guy whose body you would have happily worshipped without asking for his name first."

"I would never."

I stare at her because she's lying.

"Okay. Okay. I did do that."

"But if I had a good man like you, I'd block out that period of my life too and deny it at every turn."

"He knows everything about me, including all the stupid shit we did."

"You told him my stupid shit too?"

Alyssa laughs. "It was more like our stupid shit. We were together for all of it."

My dad stalks into the bar and stops when his eyes land on Alyssa and me sitting at a table. "I'm here. You two can go."

"What?" I ask, pushing myself up from the table. "It's my night to cover the bar."

"Alyssa's in town, and you're not going to spend a Friday night working. Go have fun. Enjoy your time together."

"You're the best, Mr. Gallo," Alyssa says, grabbing her serving tray off the table before climbing to her feet.

I get up too, going over to him to give him a kiss on the cheek. "You deserve a night off too, Dad."

He smiles down at me with the same sweetness he's shown me his entire life. I know every time he looks at me, he sees my mother. How could he not? It's as if the universe hit copy, paste, and poof, I was born. "Life's short, kid, and you two deserve to have a good time while she's visiting. Lucio's coming in tonight to help too. We've got this covered."

"Are you sure?" I ask.

"Completely."

I love my dad. He's been to hell and back—losing his wife and raising two kids on his own for a handful of years until Tilly changed everything.

He was never bitter or angry, always putting our needs before his own. I don't know what I did to deserve growing up with such a loving and patient man, but I know I hit the dad jackpot the day I was born.

"You really are the best," I tell him, repeating Alyssa's statement.

"Yeah, yeah," he mutters, never fully understanding how much Brax and I appreciate him for being our rock after everything we went through with him, too.

"You know what I want to do tonight?" Alyssa asks as we head toward the back room to grab our purses.

"What?"

"A tattoo. You game?"

"You want me to do it?"

"Are your skills shit?"

"No," I tell her.

I'd always loved art and drawing, but I never thought about being a tattoo artist until I spent some time in Florida with my cousins. There was something about their shop Inked that I fell absolutely in love with.

The last time I went for a visit, I decided there was nothing else I wanted to do. Bar life wasn't for me, and I couldn't bake a cupcake to save my life. I talked to my cousins about opening a branch of their shop on the South-side of Chicago, and when they agreed, I jumped in feet-first without a second thought.

And as a bonus, they take turns coming to visit for special guest spots at the shop to tattoo some of the people in the neighborhood. It's a win-win for everyone. I even converted the top floor of the shop to an apartment for when they're here.

But what I didn't know when I came up with the idea to do tattoos was how rigorous the training would be. My tech-nique was crap for a few years, but every day, I got better.

Luckily, I have amazing artists who rent chairs at the shop, driving lots of traffic and helping build the business quicker than I would've been able to do alone.

"But they're not the best either."

"Can you trace handwriting?"

"I can do that." It was the most basic and easiest thing for me to do. I spent years forging my dad's signature. Who knew that talent would come in handy years later?

Alyssa pulls a small photo out of her purse and hands it to me. "I want what's written on the back to be tattooed on my arm."

The picture is of her father when he served in the mili-tary. The man was handsome when he was young. Strong jaw, full head of hair, and could fill out a uniform nicely. When I flip it over, a few words are scribbled on the back.

At least I'm not lost.

"You want this?" I ask her, glancing up from the paper.

She nods. "Ever since he passed away, I've wanted to get those words put on my skin in his handwriting. A permanent reminder of him."

"If this is what you want, I can make it happen."

"There's no one I trust with this more than you."

"You obviously need to get your head checked, then."

Alyssa laughs and smacks my arm. "If you mess it up, I'll never let you forget it."

"If I mess it up, at least you live in Georgia, and I won't have to look at it every day."

"You're a jerk," she mutters, shaking her head.

"But you love me."

She sighs loudly. "I do and always will."

Besides my family, Alyssa has been the only other constant in my life. She's my ride-or-die. She knows everything about me—every mistake, every secret, every heartbreak.

One of the saddest days of my life was when she decided to go to college in Georgia and then fell in love with a local, giving me no hope of her ever moving back to Chicago.

"Afterward, we'll find some trouble," she says, her eyes twinkling with all the possibilities.

"I don't know if I have the energy for that tonight, babe."

She stares at me with her lips flat. "You don't have the energy for fun?"

I shrug, wishing I'd taken a nap earlier today. I worked at the shop way too late last night, but I didn't want to leave until Timber finished his last tattoo. "We'll figure it out after we're done."

"Hey. What was the third thing on your list of promises you made yourself when you turned thirty?"

I glance around, making sure there isn't anyone nearby. "No more hookups without a relationship first."

"Oh boy. That's going to be interesting."

"So far, I've been able to do it."

"You turned thirty last week, sweetheart. Don't pat yourself on the back too much for making it seven whole days without a one-night stand."

I give her my middle finger before heading to the shop to do a tattoo and maybe find a little bit of trouble afterward.

CHAPTER 4
WYLDER

"THEY'LL BE FINE, Wylder. Go blow off some steam," Ma says as she pushes me toward her front door. "I think the three of you need a break from one another for the night. I'll talk to the girls about what happened today and explain why it was wrong."

"Don't you think I should be the one to talk to them?"

She shakes her head as she twists her lips. "No. Not while you're still upset."

I stare down into my mom's deep brown eyes, wondering how she has the patience of a saint. "Why aren't you more upset?"

The laughter that bubbles out of my mom is unlike anything I've heard in a long time. "You clearly don't remember what a little shit you were when you were young. You did way worse things. I don't even know how I survived. I swear you were trying to put me in an early grave."

"I'm sorry," I say quickly, feeling more than a little guilty for being a dumbass, boneheaded teenager.

"And to be honest, you still scare the crap out of me most nights. I worry about you." She lifts her hand to my cheek, cradling my face like she did when I was a little boy. "You've been through just as much as they have, and someday, you're going to pop once it all hits you."

"It's been four years, Ma. It's hit me. Pop averted."

"That's a lot of days of anger building up inside you. You think you've popped, but I don't think you have."

I peer over my mother's shoulder to where the girls are perched on her couch with a giant bowl of popcorn between them. They're totally engrossed in the movie she put on for them and not paying any attention to us.

Maddox is too busy being mad at me to even look in my direction. She thinks I overreacted about her trip down the street to the local bar, while I think I handled it well, barely raising my voice.

"You almost lost your cool today with the girls, and I know that's not you, Wylder. You're the best dad I've ever known, but they almost pushed you over the edge. What they did was bad, but they're okay and safe."

I run my fingers through my hair, trying not to chastise myself too harshly for being a second away from losing my temper.

I wasn't even mad until Maddy stepped foot on the porch and didn't look the least bit guilty about the panic she'd caused by disappearing into thin air without us having any way to find them.

For a year now, she's begged for a cell phone, and I've been vehement in my response that it isn't happening until she is at least sixteen. But today, when we didn't know where they were, a cell phone would've made things a lot easier.

"Maybe I need to get Maddy a phone," I whisper to my mom, because although they don't look like they're listening, I know those girls hear everything.

"That would be smart. You can't keep her a little girl forever, Wylder. She's going to need a way to call for help if she's stranded or wanders away again."

"She better not wander away again."

My mom gently wraps her hand around my wrist, giving me a light squeeze. "Things aren't going to get easier. She's growing up quickly and will test her boundaries daily."

"Fuckin' great," I mutter, remembering doing the same thing without putting any thought into how it made my parents feel.

Ma laughs again, loving that I'm about to be paid back for all my antics when I was younger.

Hazel's the one who follows all the rules, always worried about doing what's right.

But Maddy...she's all me, and I know without a shadow of a doubt that I have a very rocky decade in front of me without a partner to lean on.

"Now, go. Get a good night's sleep and come by for breakfast and to get the girls."

"Are you sure, Ma? That's a lot for you."

Her eyes narrow as she peers up at me. "I may be older, honey, but I'm not dead. I can still cook a meal for my family with this old body."

I lift my hands, hating that I made her feel bad. "I know, Ma, but it was a stressful day."

"There's no better way for me to unwind than to hang out with my grandkids. You, on the other hand, need something a little different."

I raise an eyebrow, and she chuckles in response.

"You're young and single. Go out and act like it."

I pinch the bridge of my nose, trying to block out the fact that my mother is implying I need to get laid. "The last thing I need is a woman in my life."

"I didn't say you should run out and get married. Also, not every woman is like Katie either. You're going to have to take a chance on someone someday, baby. You're too young to spend the rest of your life alone."

"It's too soon for the girls."

She makes a noise in the back of their throat. "Stop making excuses. The girls could use a woman in their life every day too. It would be good for all three of you."

I grumble under my breath because that's the last thing we need.

"Granny, come watch the movie with us," Hazel says, her mouth full of popcorn and in the process of grabbing another handful.

"I'm coming, sweetie. Just saying goodbye to your dad."

"Bye, Daddy," Hazel calls out, giving me a little wave with her popcorn-filled fist.

I stalk across the room, dropping a kiss on top of Hazel's head. "Sweet dreams tonight, baby."

"Always," she whispers, giving me the sweetest smile.

I lean over to give Maddox a kiss, and when I plant one on her, she doesn't throw me a sweet smile like Hazel. She also doesn't tell me to fuck off, so it's progress.

"See you girls in the morning. I love you."

"Love you too, Daddy," Hazel replies.

"Bye," Maddox says, which, again, is better than telling me to kick rocks.

I give my mother a kiss on the cheek and then head for the door, trying to leave all the stress of the day behind me.

———

"Hey, handsome. How can I make you feel good tonight?" Daisy, a regular at the bar, asks, sliding her hand across my shoulders and tracing the lines of my muscles with her fingertips.

"Nothing, Daisy. I'm good," I tell her, wanting to be kind to her but not wanting to sleep with her. She's not a bad person and she's pretty, but she's been ridden more times than the El.

"Come on, Wylder. Take Daisy for a ride," Shadow tells me as his hungry eyes travel down her body. "You're wound tighter than a roll of duct tape."

I stare at him, wondering how his brain works. "Why don't you? I think you could use it more than me."

"I'm game," Daisy says, not giving two single shits who gets her off, as long as it happens.

Shadow stands, taking Daisy's hand when she stretches her arm out. "What are you going to do, brother?"

"I'm going to go home and crash. It was a long day."

Shadow's face scrunches in disgust, or maybe it's disappointment. "Man, you sure as hell got old in a hurry. I never thought I'd see the day when my little brother grew into an old fucking person before I did."

I can't argue with him. I've been feeling like I'm a million years old lately. Being a single father isn't easy, and finding the right balance between work, family, and having a personal life is a challenge. I still haven't figured it out, and it's been over four years since Katie walked out the door on me and the girls.

"I won't always be like this."

"No. You'll only get older. Time's passing you by, Wylder."

I chew on that statement. I am wasting the best years of my life avoiding anything that may end in the same deceit as my marriage.

What am I doing?

Is my mom right? Do the girls need a woman in their life as much as I do? Is my decision to stay single because I'm too scared, or because I'm trying to protect them?

"Later, Gramps," Shadow says, slapping my shoulder before he stalks away with a very scantily clad Daisy.

I sit there for a moment, turning the beer bottle in my hand, thinking about the future. It's time for me to move forward, but I feel frozen.

I've sulked for way too long about the way my marriage ended, and I am bitter about the entire thing. I never thought Katie would cheat on me and be willing to move across the country, leaving us all behind.

Move on, Wylder.

I'm not in love with Katie anymore either. Even if she showed up on my doorstep, begging to come back, I'd slam the door right in her face.

All the feelings I'd had for her had faded away a long time ago. I am angry and bitter for the girls, not myself. They are the innocents in this, and they know their mother left them to start another family with someone else. She deserves to step on a Lego every single day to feel a small portion of the pain she inflicted on our girls and continues to do so.

"Wylder, get your ass over here," Thumper calls out across the bar as I stand to leave.

"Shit," I mutter under my breath.

"Hey," I say, giving him the standard chin lift. "What's up? I was just about to dip."

"Stick around and drink with me. You always leave so quickly. Mom said she had the kids, so you have all night."

"I'm not in the mood," I tell my brother.

"What's up your ass?" he asks, removing his arm from around his flavor of the month's shoulders.

I tilt my head, not liking his tone. "What's up my ass?" I repeat his statement, wanting to see if he'll change his words.

"Well, it's good to know your hearing works, even if your dick doesn't."

The rage I felt earlier today crawls up my spine. "Excuse me?" I seethe as my heart starts to beat faster and my blood heats. No one can piss me off more than Thumper. Since he's the oldest kid in the family, he felt it was his personal mission in life to pick on all of us. He'd toughen us up before anyone else in the world got their hands on us.

"Thumper, stop," the woman he's with begs him. "Leave him be. Your brother's a nice guy with a broken heart."

"Fuck that. He's had four years to sit in his misery and act like a little bitch. That time is over. It's time for this pansy-ass to reenter the land of the living."

"Fuck you," I spit, ready for the brawl that's going to happen no matter what I do.

He's itching for a fight, and tonight, I'm caught in his crosshairs.

Whatever.

It won't be the first time I've been punched by him, and I'm pretty sure it won't be the last. And before I know it, a fist is barreling through the air, making contact with the side of my face.

Game on.

CHAPTER 5
TATE

ALYSSA STARES DOWN at her arm, and my stomach twists as I wait to see if she's happy with the tattoo or not. She's the last person I want to disappoint.

Timber strides over and stops next to Alyssa, looking down at the tattoo with his critical gaze. "Not too bad there, Tate. The lines are crisp, and you didn't go too deep. I'm impressed."

That's a huge compliment coming from Timber. He's one of the best tattoo artists in the city, and when I opened the shop, he was chomping at the bit to rent a chair. He lives in a building on the next block and wanted to be able to roll out of bed and walk to work.

"Thanks, Timber," I say, unable to stop my smile.

Alyssa glances up at him, and their eyes meet.

If she weren't married, I'd swear those two would hook up. He's a tall drink of water and every bit of Alyssa's type, with tattoos everywhere, dark hair, deep brown eyes, and lips that I could only describe as kissable.

"I'm headed out. Need anything before I go?" he asks

as he wipes his hands with a paper towel before tossing it in the trash.

"No. We're good. I'm going to clean up and be out of here in an hour or so."

"An hour?" Alyssa asks, her eyes big.

"Yeah, babe. I have to sanitize my station and all the fun stuff a business owner does every night when they close up shop."

"You stayin' at Tate's place while you're here?" Timber asks her.

Alyssa nods. "For one more night. I head back tomorrow afternoon."

"I can walk you back on my way home."

I raise my eyebrow as I glance his way. He lives the opposite direction of my house, and it most certainly is not on his way home.

"That would be great. Do you mind, Tate?" Alyssa asks me, already moving to get her purse.

"We have to cover that first," I tell her, dipping my eyes to the fresh tattoo on her arm.

"I'll do it," Timber offers, and Alyssa's a little too eager to follow him toward his workstation.

"Thanks, Timber. You are so sweet for doing this," Alyssa says to him, gushing a bit too much. "Do you think my husband will like this?"

At least she drops those words in front of him. If Timber had any hopes of getting a piece from Alyssa before, she just killed that fantasy.

As I pass by the window, I freeze. Wylder's stalking down the street and sporting what looks like a new black eye. He stops, glances over, and our eyes lock.

My breath catches in my throat from the intensity of his

stare. "Oh shit," I whisper, unable to look away from him or get my feet unstuck from the ceramic tile.

Without an ounce of thought, I raise my hand and wave.

What the hell is wrong with me?

Wylder's hawkish stare softens immediately.

Dumb, girl. Dumb.

Two seconds later, he comes through the door of the shop and is standing in front of me. The guy is so big, he creates a shadow over me, blocking out the bright overhead lights.

"Hey," I say, drawing out the word and sounding way too chipper for a moment like this, especially with him. "Did you want some ink?"

He shakes his head, and I brace myself, waiting for him to say something totally shitty about what happened earlier. He doesn't seem to be the type of guy to do small talk and pleasantries.

However, there's nothing but silence, and it fills the room like a blanket of thick smoke.

"Um, what happened to your eye?" I ask, filling that void of quiet. I reach up, not thinking that maybe the man doesn't want to be touched.

He grabs my wrist, stopping me from touching the tender skin. I don't even know why I did it. It's not like anyone wants someone poking at their wounds, but I couldn't stop myself.

His grip is surprisingly gentle, and I fully expect him to drop my hand, but he doesn't. "What are you doing?" he asks, his voice gravelly.

"I don't know," I whisper, staring up into his blue eyes. "It looks painful, though."

"And that made you want to touch it?"

I shrug, not even the littlest bit concerned that he's still touching me. "I wanted to see how bad it is."

"I've had worse," he admits, and I have no doubt that he's telling the truth.

"What's going on?" Alyssa asks, stalking toward us with her high heels clicking against the floor.

Wylder uncurls his fingers, letting my arm go immediately.

"Nothing. Just talking to Wylder."

Alyssa's eyes widen as soon as I utter his name. "Hazel and Maddox's dad?" she asks, but she already knows, and she's already soaking him in.

"Yep," Wylder bites out. "Those are my girls."

"They're sweet girls," Alyssa tells him. "Did you need something?"

"We were just having a conversation," I reply. "Are you two heading out?"

"Maybe I'll stick around," she says, looking between Wylder and me. "Help you lock up and shit."

"No. I got it. Go back and pack. I'll be there soon," I tell her.

"Behave," Alyssa tells Wylder. "And if she doesn't come home, I'm heading right to Cheryl's after I go to the cops."

"I'm not here to hurt her."

"I tried to touch his eye," I explain.

Alyssa wrinkles her nose, and she gawks at me. "Why the hell would you do that?"

"I don't know," I whisper through clenched teeth.

"That good old impulse control seems to be slipping," she tells me with a smirk.

I know what she's talking about. Maybe she feels the snap, crackle, pop of the air between Wylder and me.

"Ready?" Timber asks Alyssa, not giving Wylder a second glance.

"I guess so," she says to him, adjusting her purse strap over her shoulder. "But only if Tate's sure."

"I am," I tell her, shooing her toward the door. "I'll be fine."

She stares at me as she moves. "Are you sure?" she whispers, glancing over my shoulder.

"I promise."

"He's fucking hot."

"I know," I say before Timber is at her side, and they leave.

I take three seconds to gather myself before I turn back around to face Wylder.

"Your name's Tate, right?"

"One and only," I say, stalking past him to get to my workstation.

"Is this your place?"

"Yep." I busy myself with cleaning, letting Wylder do whatever Wylder is going to do.

"It's impressive," he says in a warmer tone.

"Thanks."

His boots echo on the tile floor as he moves around the shop. "I wanted to thank you for earlier."

"It was nothing."

"It was something to me, Tate."

I glance up when he says my name. I like how it sounds coming out of his mouth, and that spells trouble for me. "I make a mean Shirley Temple."

Wylder blows out a loud breath before collapsing into one of the waiting room chairs. "I'm glad they wandered into your place and not some of the other bars around here."

If I thought he looked large standing, he looks even bigger sitting down. His legs seem to stretch out farther than I'd ever think humanly possible.

"They were safe. No one bothered them, and we all love Cheryl too."

"I didn't know my mom went to bars."

"She comes in once or twice a week for a bite to eat and company. She's been doing it for years since her husband died."

"She misses Dad a lot, but I never would've guessed she'd go to a bar when she's lonely."

"We're more than a bar. My family's owned it for almost fifty years, and everyone's more like family than customers. She's in good hands with us, and your girls were too."

"I don't know what the hell I'm doing anymore," he admits in a moment of vulnerability as he stares down the length of his legs. "I think I'm fucking everything up."

I stop what I'm doing, wanting to give him my full attention. It's not that I care about him, but I liked his girls, and I know what a difficult time they must be having without their mom around.

"Why do you think that?" I ask, setting down the cleaning supplies and moving toward the waiting room to where he looks way sadder than I'd ever imagine possible.

"I wasn't built to be a single father to two little girls. I don't know anything about girly shit."

I can't stop the tiny laugh from escaping my lips, earning me a glance from Wylder. "Sorry," I tell him and clear my throat before sliding into a chair, leaving one between us. "It doesn't matter if they're girls or boys, kids only want to know you love them."

"How would you know?"

I search his eyes, hating that I'm going to get into my personal life, which I don't do often, but I feel like it's important at a time like this. "My mom died when I was young. My dad didn't plan on being a single father to two kids either, but he survived, and so did we."

"Fuck," he hisses, his eyes softening and remorseful. "I'm so sorry."

"It's okay," I say, my typical answer when someone finds out my mother died when I was little.

"I love them more than anything else in this world. It's so hard watching them be sad every day, and there's nothing I can do to fix it."

I turn my body, bending my knee to put my ankle underneath me. "Wylder, you can't fix everything, but you can put on a good show every day. If you're happy, they'll be happy."

"It's that easy?"

"Are you happy every day?" I ask him, but I already know the answer.

"Is anyone?"

"Nope, but you can fake it until you make it. Girls need love…lots of love. Kisses and hugs. Since they don't have a mom, they need their dad. They need to know you're not going to leave too."

His face morphs into something akin to horror. "I would never do that."

"I'm sure they thought that about their mom at some point too."

"Katie's trash."

"Katie," I whisper-hiss.

"Hazel's easy to shower love on, but Maddox is another situation." He squeezes his eyes shut, letting his head fall backward until it makes contact with the wall.

I smile, remembering her attitude earlier. "Teenagers suck."

"Please tell me she'll grow out of it in a year?"

"How old is she?"

"Fourteen."

I burst into laughter. "You have about ten years of this Maddox before a different one takes over."

"Jesus," he mutters, curling his hands around the metal arms of the chair. "I won't survive."

"You will, but it's going to be rocky."

"I know nothing about teenage girls."

"You were once a teenage boy, yeah?"

I try to imagine what a teenage Wylder would have been like, but I draw a complete blank. Did he always look like he stewed in anger all day? Did he sprout after high school, or was he one of those boys who had a full beard by the time they hit sophomore year?

"Times were different then, and it was a long, long time ago."

"How long?" I ask, prying for no reason except personal curiosity.

Stop getting personal, Tate. He's off-limits. He's a biker dude and a single dad.

"I'm forty-three."

I rock back with that admission. "Wow."

"Wow, as in I'm ancient as hell, or wow, you look amazing, Wylder?"

I can't stop a smile from spreading across my face at the playfulness in his question. "You look great. I wouldn't have guessed a day over thirty-five."

"Shit, I'll take that compliment, but I know you're lying. I think I look like I'm a hundred—or at least I feel like I'm that old."

"You do act like a crotchety old man."

His lips flatten. "There hasn't been much to feel young about lately."

"Your kids would disagree."

He sighs as his shoulders sag forward. "What do I do?"

"Take the girls out this week. Go roller-skating or biking. Get out and enjoy our big, beautiful city."

"Maddox would rather chew her arm off than go skating or biking. She's not into anything physical or outdoors."

"How about taking them to the Mag Mile for some shopping?"

He scrubs his hand down his face and grunts. "That sounds like torture."

"A little bit of torture on your end this weekend will go a long way to melting Maddox's icy teenage exterior."

"I know nothing about that area. Which shops do kids like?"

I take in his outfit, which clearly didn't come from any designer stores. "There are a bunch."

"Not helpful," he grumbles.

"Want me to make a list?" I offer for whatever reason. If he were my dad and I were those girls, I'd hope someone would do the same.

"You don't need to do that."

"Give me your number," I say, taking my phone out of the back pocket of my jeans, "and I'll text you some ideas later once I'm done cleaning."

He stares at me for a beat before he says, "Okay." He rattles off his phone number, and I store it in my contacts under M for Moody and Broody.

"I promise you'll have a list by morning."

"Thanks," he murmurs genuinely.

I stand back up, heading toward my station to get back to cleaning. "So, you want to tell me what happened to your face?"

"Will it make you happy? Because it's not that interesting of a story."

"It will at least pass the time while I finish up here, and maybe the story will be a little entertaining too."

"Some asshole I know sucker-punched me."

"What did you do to deserve it?"

"He called me a bitch and told me it was time for me to stop sulking and reenter the land of the living, so I told him to fuck off."

I stop what I'm doing and stare at the spot on his face that will look worse tomorrow. "That's all? You said fuck off? Did you at least get in a shot too?"

"A few."

"Any good ones?"

"He was the one lying on the floor when I left." Wylder smiles. "He deserved it too."

"Did he throw the first punch?"

"Yep, but not the last."

"Way to go. Feel better now?"

"No."

"No?" I ask as I toss the dirty paper towels in the trash. "Should I?"

"Not really. I don't think violence is a healthy way to deal with your feelings."

"Do you have any idea how long it's been since I've punched someone—or been punched, for that matter?"

I shake my head, but I assume it hasn't been that long because he's a man who looks like he'd use his fists to solve a lot of his issues. "No idea."

"It's been more than a decade."

I rock back on the heels of my favorite lace-up black boots. "Really?"

"Is it that surprising?"

"Kind of."

"I know how I look," he says, rubbing his hands together as he looks away from me. "I look like I throw punches all the time, but I'm a dad and I used to be a husband. I have responsibilities, and I'm an adult. I know how to use my words without resorting to violence."

"Well then, I'm glad you laid the guy out. He deserved it."

Wylder cracks a smile for the first time, and it makes my heart go pitter-patter in my chest. If I thought the man was handsome when he looked menacing, he is drop-dead gorgeous when he seems happy. "I better run and let you finish up. Thanks for your help, Tate."

"Anytime, Wylder," I say, continuing to clean up. I didn't want to make the goodbye awkward. "I'll get you that list, and I hope you and the girls have fun tomorrow."

"I look forward to hearing from you," he says before he heads toward the door.

I try to stop from checking out his ass, but I can't help myself, and it's a fine ass too.

Shocker.

He glances over his shoulder as his hands touch the handle, and he catches me looking. Fuck.

CHAPTER 6
WYLDER

THE MOMENT my boots touch the sidewalk, I regret leaving so quickly. I should've stayed and walked her to her car, making sure she got there safely. She did as much for my girls, and it's the least I can do, instead of leaving her alone when the streets are unusually empty.

But if I am honest with myself, it's the first time I've felt that kind of pull toward a woman in a very long time.

Fuck it.

I turn and stare at her through the window. She moves around the shop, her mouth opening and closing like she's having a full conversation with someone, but I know she's alone.

I wonder what she's saying. Is it about me?

It isn't lost on me that she checked out my ass as I walked out the door. I know I'm not the only one who felt the air in the room change when she came closer to me.

The entire time we talked, I fantasized about grabbing her, holding her in my arms, and kissing her full lips. But I stopped myself.

Maybe Thumper is right. I am a pansy. The old me wouldn't have stopped until I tasted her mouth.

This me, the one who had my heart shattered, does everything I can to avoid feeling anything other than disappointment.

But before I know it, my feet are moving me forward, and I reach for the handle, tearing the door open, and march back into the shop.

Tate's head snaps upward, and our eyes meet. "Did you forget something?"

"One thing." I close the space between us with a few long strides.

When she angles her head back to look up at me, I slide my hand around the side of her neck and pull her closer.

She gasps as our bodies collide, and the feel of her against me is better than I could have imagined.

I snake my other arm around her back until her hair is in my hands, pulling her head farther backward until I have complete control of her.

"This," I whisper before taking her lips with mine.

I didn't bother asking if it's okay.

Tonight, I am more in the mood to beg for forgiveness than ask for permission.

I want this.

I need this.

The crackle in the air from earlier is back but now stronger than before. My knees almost go weak from the softness of her lips and the intoxicating perfume she's wearing.

I tug on her ponytail, and she moans, the vibrations going straight to my dick.

There are no other sounds in the shop besides our

heavy, labored breathing and our lips devouring each other.

I could get lost in this moment and stay here forever, but it's impossible. Even if this is all there will ever be, I couldn't let the opportunity pass by without shooting my shot.

My body comes alive with her in my arms. I forgot how good it feels to kiss someone...to get lost in them.

Everything fades away as she slides her arms around my back, tethering herself to me.

I pull back, knowing we're entering dangerous territory because it's been years since I've kissed a woman with this much passion and need.

She gazes up at me with lazy eyes, puffy lips, and gasping for air.

"What the..." Her voice trails off as she blinks away the haze of lust.

I concentrate on my breathing, still holding her tightly with my hand wrapped around her hair. "I needed to see."

"Needed to see what?"

"If what I felt was real."

"Was it?" she whispers, her eyes searching mine.

"Yeah, baby. It was for me."

I shouldn't have kissed her. I shouldn't have let my impulses take me over without any thought.

She's the type of woman where one taste isn't enough.

Now, I want to spend hours exploring her body, losing myself in her softness and warmth.

Shit.

This isn't good.

"I got to go," I tell her before releasing my grip on her and stalking out the door.

Maybe I am a pansy, like Thumper said earlier. I should stay or maybe apologize, but that's never been my style.

I barely make it fifteen feet down the sidewalk when I hear, "Hey!"

I turn, finding Tate on the sidewalk with her fingers tracing her bottom lip. I fully expect her to tell me off, call me an asshole, or march right up to me and give me a matching black eye on the other side.

But that's not what she does. She barrels toward me, sprinting at full speed, and I open my arms, knowing she's about to collide with me.

She leaps into my arms, wrapping her legs and arms around me. Nothing else is said as she smashes her mouth down on mine, taking my lips harder than I did hers.

I slide my hands under her bottom, holding the entirety of her weight as her tongue strokes the seam of my lips. I can't stop myself from giving it all to her, wanting her more than the air I breathe.

My head is swimming with a world of possibilities as I squeeze her ass, and our tongues tangle together. My cock strains against the rough material of my jeans, an unfamiliar sensation for me the last few years.

I want her.

I want her more than I've wanted anyone.

And suddenly, she pulls away, climbing down my body like she's done it a million times before. It's my turn to be in a haze. "What was that?" I ask, gasping for air and trying to find my footing because Tate puts me totally off-kilter.

"I needed to see if it was real."

"Was it?" I ask her, repeating her same question from a minute ago.

"Yeah," she says and pokes me in the chest with her long fingernail. "But don't you ever walk out without saying goodbye, asshole." And with those words, she spins on the heels of her boots and stalks back to her shop without giving me another look.

Damn.

If I wasn't in lust before, I sure as fuck am now, and I know nothing but trouble lies ahead.

Just before midnight, my phone beeps.

Unknown: Here's the list. Good luck.

The text is followed by ten places I've never heard of, much less know where they are.

I stare at the message for a solid minute before I decide to answer. I don't like how we left things earlier. Neither of us handled the situation like an adult, but that hasn't stopped me from smiling every time I think about the way she stalked off, leaving me in the dust.

Me: Am I about to be broke?

Unknown: Probably.

I take a minute to store her name in my phone. I didn't want the conversation to end as abruptly as our kiss.

Me: Sorry about earlier.

Tate: You should be.

Damn. This girl has attitude, and for some odd reason, I like it. Maybe it's because she's honest even when it's brutal.

Me: I freaked out and had to walk out when I shouldn't have.

Tate: At least you realize your mistake.

Me: Kissing you wasn't a mistake, though.

Tate: You know what I'm talking about.

I scrub my hand across my face, trying to think of what to say next. I've never been much of a small-talker, and flirting via text is not something I'm used to doing.

Small talk.

I can do it.

I have to if I want to get anywhere with someone like Tate—or any woman, for that matter. I can't dazzle her with my dick alone.

Women want more, expect it nowadays.

My mind goes to our conversation earlier about her mother and father.

Me: Did your dad ever remarry?

I wince as soon as I hit send and decide to send another message in case she doesn't want to talk about what happened after her mother passed.

Me: You can tell me to fuck off.

It's not long before three dots appear on the screen. I wait, staring at my phone to see which way she goes with her answer.

I don't know why I even asked that question. I guess I want to know I might have a chance. That, even at my age, I can find love again.

Tate: Yeah. He met Tilly a few years after Mom passed away. She owns the bakery next to the bar.

I know the place. I've taken the girls in there more than once. It was a must every time we came to visit my mom, and now that we live closer, we go there once a week and on special occasions.

Me: I know the place. The girls love it.

Tate: Only weirdos don't like cupcakes and cookies.

I smile at her statement. I've always thought the same, but I've wondered if I am the weirdo for thinking it.

Me: Did you like her?

My fear of falling in love is that the girls will hate the woman. Things are already bad enough, and adding someone the girls don't like would be an absolute disaster.

Tate: We loved her from the moment we met her, but she loved us too. If a woman doesn't treat your kids like the little princesses they are, run the other way.

Me: Noted.

I also make a mental note about how Tate treated the girls earlier when she walked them back to my mom's house. The way her eyes lit up when she talked about them with me or complimented me on how cute and sweet they are.

Tate: Tilly's always treated me like a daughter, and because of that, I've always thought of her as a mom.

That gives me hope that all isn't lost. Maddox is at an important time in her development and needs a female in her life under the age of sixty. My mom does her best, but she grew up in a different era and has a hard time understanding what Maddox's life is like.

Hell, I barely understand either.

Tate: Is your ex involved in their lives?

I swallow down the anger about what Katie's done to our girls.

Me: Not really.

Tate: Shameful.

Me: That's one word for her behavior.

Tate: When was the last time they saw her?

Me: A year ago. She came to town for a family funeral and visited the girls for one day.

Tate: It took a funeral for her to see her kids?

Me: Yep.

Tate: Awful.

Me: She's that too.

Tate: Is she coming back soon?

Me: Nope.

Tate: I hate her.

Me: Same.

Tate: My mother fought so hard for her life, suffering because she wanted to be here for us. And your ex...she just walked out the door without a single thought about what it would do to her kids. How does a woman abandon them?

Me: She's selfish, but she always was.

Tate: What happened? I know I'm being nosy, and you can totally tell me you don't want to talk about it.

Me: She'd been having an affair at work for years without me knowing, and when he was transferred, she dropped the bomb on me that she was in love with someone else and going with him too.

Tate: Harsh.

Me: He has money, and that's more important to her than anything else, including our kids.

Tate: She'll be sorry someday.

Me: Probably not. She'll be rolling in dough for the rest of her life, which wouldn't have happened if she'd stayed here with us.

I do well for myself, but by no means am I well-off. My

girls want for nothing and I have no debt, but I didn't have the income to buy Katie designer clothes and extravagant jewelry.

I spend my days restoring classic cars and reselling them for a hefty profit. Sometimes I get lucky and find a rare gem for a steal and turn it for a mind-blowing amount of cash. But I never spend it all, knowing I'll need money to send the girls to college someday, or God forbid, if the classic car market ever dries up.

Tate: Money isn't everything. I know my father would've given up every dollar he had if it meant my mother could've lived longer.

Me: Most men would do the same, and if they wouldn't, they aren't worth shit.

When I'd thought Katie loved me, I would've burned down the world to protect her and the girls. I would've jumped in front of a bullet to keep her breathing, without hesitating for a single second. What an idiot.

Tate: I'm sorry to do this, but Alyssa is waiting on me. Have fun on your shopping spree with the girls.

I chew on my lip, wondering if…maybe…

Me: Are you interested in joining us?

The worst thing she can say is no, right? It's not like I'm asking her on a date.

Me: I don't know any of the places, and I'm sure the girls would love to have a female's opinion on things. Plus, I wouldn't get lost trying to find all the stores.

There's a pause, and I hold my breath, staring at the phone.

Tate: I'm busy tomorrow, but I'm free Sunday.

Me: Sunday it is.

Tate: Talk tomorrow.

Me: Night.

Tate: Good night, Wylder.

I finally release the breath I've been holding for way too long.

She said yes, and for the first night in a long time, things are looking up.

CHAPTER 7
TATE

ALYSSA CURLS up on the couch next to me and nudges me with her shoulder. "What happened after I left?"

"Nothing," I tell her, staring out the living room window at the faint glow of the light from downtown.

"Wylder is fine, girl. He wasn't at all what I was expecting."

"He's cute," I say, doing my best to keep my voice flat.

"Is he a good kisser?"

I turn my head to the side and stare at her. "Why do you ask that?"

She reaches her hand out, pressing her index finger into the skin near my lip. "You have beard burn."

I hang my head in shame. "I didn't mean for it to happen."

"Did he kiss you, or did you kiss him?" She lifts the wineglass to her lips and waits for the answer.

"The first time, he kissed me."

"And the second?" she asks without missing a beat.

"I kissed him."

"Start at the beginning. I want to know everything, and you better not leave a detail out."

And so, I do. I tell her everything. I explain how Wylder confided in me, letting his guard drop long enough to share how he feels about being a single father. I tell her how he left, came back in, and grabbed me before I had a chance to react.

"But was it a good kiss?"

I nod slowly as I think back over how it all happened. "Too good."

"Goodbye, birthday promise," she says and laughs. "It was stupid anyway. Don't make rules that could stop you from having a good time. You only live once, and life's too short to deprive yourself of something or someone you crave."

"Technically, he breaks one of the rules but not all of them. I don't plan on sleeping with him, but he is a biker."

"Is he a biker, or does he ride a bike?"

I shrug. "Honestly, I don't know. We didn't talk about any of that. Only his girls, his struggles as a single dad, and what my family went through with losing my mom."

"You shared that with him?"

"Yeah."

Alyssa sets down her wineglass on the coffee table in front of us before grabbing my hand. "You don't share that with many strangers, Tate. I'd say that's a big deal."

"Maybe."

Is it a big deal? I didn't think it was.

Most people in my life know about my mom dying, and it's not something you bring up in casual conversation with a stranger. No one wants to hear the sad girl talk about her dead mom. It's a good-time killer.

"It's interesting that he didn't talk about his bike. That's pretty telling."

I stretch out my legs, propping my feet on the coffee table next to her wine before placing my hands behind my head. "What's it say?"

"It says he has a bike but isn't a biker. It says it's not his only personality unlike Rowdy."

I let my head loll toward her. "You think?"

"Tell me a time Rowdy didn't talk about the brotherhood."

"It's all he wanted to talk about when he wasn't balls deep inside me."

"The man had two obsessions—pussy and his club."

"That's no lie," I say before giggling. "What the hell did I see in him?"

"Orgasms," she says flatly. "Thanks to a magical tongue, from what you've said."

"Fingers and cock too." I shake my head, remembering the man used to make me scream. "But I still don't know if it was worth all the hassle in the end."

"Yeah, death would be a pretty hefty price to pay when you could give yourself the same experience with a vibrator."

"It's so not the same."

"Can I tell you something?" she asks me, grabbing her wine again like she needs the liquid courage for whatever she's about to divulge.

"Anything. I thought we didn't have any secrets, babe."

She frowns and stares down at her glass while she traces the rim with her free hand. "It's embarrassing."

"I know you shit your pants in fifth grade while we were in gym class. Can it be worse than that?"

"That was the worst. Thank God no one noticed."

"It's a good thing we snuck out the back door before anyone did. It was totally worth the three days of detention for our disappearing act."

"Thanks for never telling anyone about that, even your dad."

"Did you shit your pants in public again?" I ask, hoping it's nothing as embarrassing as that. It's bad enough when you do it as a kid, but having it happen as an adult would be horrifying.

"Carter has never given me an orgasm."

My mouth drops open. Carter is her husband. He looks like a capable man, and I know Alyssa has the ability because she slept with more than her fair share of guys before she met him. "For real?" I whisper.

She nods as she keeps her eyes down like she can't bear to face me. "I've tried, and so has he. God, he's been relentless in the pursuit of giving me one. To the point that now I feel more pressure than ever."

"Damn," I mutter under my breath. "You at least have a vibrator or something, right?"

She nods again. "Yeah, and we use it together, but he feels like he's letting me down."

"Is he?"

"Hell no. The man does magical things to my body, but now the pressure's too much that it could never happen."

"I don't think many men realize it's a mental thing for

us. The more pressure we're under, the less likely we'll be able to get there."

"I'm going to talk to him when I get home and hope he doesn't freak out. It's really been a problem in our marriage. He feels like a failure, and I'm exhausted both mentally and physically from trying to make it happen so he can move on to something else."

"How did he even find out? I mean, when I can't get off with someone, I fake it like I'm trying to win an award from Hollywood, and guys can't tell the difference."

"I used to, but then I confessed in a couples therapy session that I had faked an orgasm because we were addressing the pressure he puts on himself, and it snowballed from there."

"I thought therapy was supposed to fix shit?" My mind is spinning from her entire confession. I never had any idea they had problems and would need therapy, especially because their relationship is still relatively new.

"I thought it would too, but it only made things worse," she says softly, sounding so unlike the Alyssa I've always known.

Her shimmer is gone. The vibrant part of her that has always been filled with laughter and light has vanished.

"Is that why you were looking at Timber like he was a snack?" I ask, trying to lighten the mood.

"His size and face weren't lost on me."

"I have an idea."

"What?" she grumbles, never liking the things I come up with because they're usually ridiculous. And this time isn't any different.

"Why don't you tie Carter to the bed and ride his face until you orgasm? Then you control the movement, the timing, and he can't do shit about it. He'd technically be the one giving you the orgasm. And if it doesn't work, you can just smother him with your pussy until he stops breathing. Either way, problem solved."

Alyssa stares at me, blinking a few times, no doubt processing the brilliance of my plan. "I don't wish him dead, Tate."

"I've heard it's a fantasy most men have. That's the way they'd like to go out. Why not make their dreams become a reality?"

"You're a complete weirdo and maybe a little psycho too."

I give her a smile. "Normal is boring."

"But," she says before taking a sip of her wine, still mulling over my idea, "I like the first part of your idea. He's always in control of everything. Maybe I could get him to go for it."

"I can't imagine he'll say no."

"He's not the same guy you met years ago. He's stressed out about everything, even grocery shopping. I'm waiting for him to die from a heart attack because of all the pressure he puts on himself."

"That doesn't sound like fun."

"Marriage is hard."

"You're not selling me on the dream, Alyssa. No orgasms. Grumpy hubby. Sounds fabulous."

"Don't listen to me. Everything is great otherwise. I mean, there're worse things than your man trying to plea-sure you every second of the day. Now, that's enough about me. Let's get back to Wylder. Are you going to see him again?"

"Sunday afternoon."

She looks at me funny. "An afternoon date?"

"It's not a date. He's taking his daughters downtown for a day of shopping, and he invited me along."

"Ooh," she sings, "That's technically a date—and a pretty big deal that he wants you around his kids."

"It's not like I haven't met them before, and the man is clueless about shopping."

"Most men are," she reminds me, even though I don't need it. "At least straight ones."

"His wardrobe didn't scream fashionista yesterday."

She waves me off as she swallows down the last of her wine. "It was screaming something else, and all of it involves a good time."

"Please tell me I'm fucking up and not to get ahead of myself," I beg her, knowing I'm going to be let down again. But this time is worse because there're kids involved. Things could get complicated in a hurry.

"Maybe you two could be friends."

"I can't be friends with a man who makes my toes curl in my boots when he kisses me."

She taps the side of her wineglass and tilts her head. "That good of a kisser, huh?"

I nod and drop my head into my hands. "This is bad, Alyssa. Really bad."

"Stop with the doom and gloom. A hot dad isn't the worst type of guy to date."

I peer up at her as my stomach twists at the thought of all the ways this could go wrong. "It makes things a hell of a lot more complicated, though."

"The mom could be a problem."

"She's washed her hands of them and moved out of state with her new guy."

Alyssa's mouth falls open in horror. "Seriously?"

"Yep."

"What kind of trash human does that?"

"Her, obviously."

"Those poor girls."

"I know," I whisper, hating how rejected they must feel. I'm sure they've gone over everything a million times, trying to figure out what they could've done differently to make her stay. It's always so easy to blame ourselves for other people's problems and mistakes.

"Well, at least you won't have to deal with her on a daily basis."

"She hasn't been here to visit in a year."

Alyssa shakes her head, making a guttural noise in the back of her throat. "If she were here, I'd punch the bitch."

"Same."

She sighs as she snuggles into the corner cushion of the couch. "I like Wylder for you."

"You don't know him."

"A single girl dad is way better than Rowdy, the biker who almost got you killed with his bullshit."

I can't argue with that.

CHAPTER 8
TATE

"ALYSSA GET OFF OKAY?" Aunt Daphne asks as I walk into the bar on Saturday night.

"Yeah," I reply, but my mind immediately goes to our conversation last night about orgasms. "Her flight was on time, for once."

She's busy cleaning a sink full of glasses and doesn't stop when I sit down across the bar from her. "I heard Wylder's kids were in here."

"You know Wylder?"

"I've known him for a long time."

"How long?"

She glances up and stops moving. "You like him?"

I stiffen and raise my chin, hating that she knows me so well. "No, I don't."

She laughs and shakes her head. "Whatever lie you want to tell yourself."

"What's going on?" Uncle Lucio asks as he walks out from the back room and overhears us.

"Nothing," I say a little too quickly.

"She likes Wylder," Daphne says, ticking her chin at me as she stares at my uncle.

Lucio's eyes widen as he comes to a stop a few feet away. "No shit. Really? Wylder?"

"I don't like him," I argue.

"She was asking about him," Daphne adds.

"Ahh. She likes him," Lucio says.

I fold my arms on top of the bar and set my head on top. "They're impossible," I mutter to the wood.

I love my family, but they're so nosy and quick to jump to conclusions. Although they aren't wrong, I will deny it until I can't anymore.

"He's a good guy. Shitty what his ex-wife did to him and their kids, but he's solid."

"She's trash. I always hated Katie. She was such a stuck-up twat," Daphne says, making me look up.

"You know her?" I ask, surprised. I shouldn't be, though. When you own a neighborhood bar, you get to know everyone in the area.

"She came in here a few times with Wylder, and I never liked her. She was rude to everyone."

"I hope you made her drinks watery," I say to my aunt.

"I did, and I didn't use the top-shelf shit like she asked for either."

"You're devious," Lucio says to her. "Totally badass."

Daphne bows with a smirk. "I learned from the best."

"What are you bowing about, Daphne?" Grandma asks as she takes the seat next to me.

"My deviousness."

"Your father taught you kids all the bad things," Grandma says as she pulls a bowl of peanuts in front of her. "Lord knows you didn't learn it from me."

Aunt Daphne stares at her mother in disbelief. "Ma, be serious. You've got a wicked streak as wide as anyone I know. It's why you and Dad are such a good match."

"I do not," Grandma says before popping a peanut into her mouth and chewing slower than any human I've ever known. "I was always so innocent before I met your father."

"Men will do that to women," Daphne adds. "I mean, Delilah was so sweet until she met Lucio."

"My wife's an angel."

"Oh, okay," Daphne teases her brother.

"Who was Daphne being mean to?" Grandma asks.

"No one lately. We were talking about something that happened a while ago," Lucio tells Grandma.

"To whom?"

"You know Wylder, Ma?" Daphne asks Grandma.

"He's a handsome devil."

Daphne snickers. "He is that."

"What about him?" Grandma asks.

Kill me now.

I already know that by the end of the day, every single person in my family will know that I asked about Wylder —including my father.

"We were talking about his ex-wife," Lucio explains.

Grandma shakes her head with a grunt. "She's a hag."

"Well, tell us how you really feel, Ma." Lucio chuckles.

"Cheryl raised some wild kids, but Wylder didn't live up to his name. He's a good kid, but his ex-wife...ugh. The worst human being," Grandma says. "I remember when his football team won State. I thought he'd end up like Vinnie and go pro."

I jerk my head back in surprise. Wylder didn't look like

the collegiate type. He has the size, but for some reason, I can't imagine him playing a high school sport. "Wylder played football?" I ask.

"He was one of the best until his brother broke his knee. Ended that poor boy's future with one dumbass kick to the leg."

"That's messed up," I whisper, feeling so bad for Wylder.

"His brothers are jerks. I never liked any of them," Daphne states. "And after that shit went down with Rowdy and those dipshits, I didn't care what neighborhood they came from. They, along with every other person in an MC, are on my shit list and banned from the bar."

"But Wylder isn't in the MC, right?" I ask, needing clarification. If he is, any thought of another kiss will quickly go out the window.

"No, baby. Wylder isn't like his brothers. He was always a family man," Grandma tells me, patting my hand with a smile. "He had his priorities straight, unlike the other boys."

"Why are we talking about Wylder?" my dad asks from behind me, scaring the ever-loving shit out of me.

"Tate was asking about him," Daphne says, and then her eyes dip to me because she knows she fucked up.

Let the Angelo Gallo inquisition begin.

"Why?" Dad asks, and I don't need to turn to know he's standing with his arms folded, feet wide apart, a scowl on his face.

"His girls came in here yesterday, and I walked them home."

"Cheryl called me about that last night to thank me.

She was so worried," Grandma says, trying to steer the conversation more toward the kids than Wylder.

"What do you mean, they were in here? And why would Cheryl be worried?" Dad asks Grandma.

I spin my stool around to face my dad, wanting to answer the question instead of Grandma. "They came in because they wanted Shirley Temples, and she didn't know where they were," I explain.

It's the truth without giving him the whole story. I don't know why I don't tell him they snuck out, but I don't want anyone to think the girls are troublemakers.

"After they had their drinks, I walked them back to Cheryl's house since she was watching them," I finish.

My dad's face softens a bit. "I remember when you loved drinking those."

"I still make myself one every once in a while...when I'm feeling nostalgic."

"I make a mean Dirty Shirley," Aunt Daphne says. "Want one?"

"A Dirty Shirley?" I ask.

She nods. "Same as the original but with a shot of vodka."

My eyebrows rise. Why didn't I ever think to do that? "Sounds delicious."

"Next girls' night, I'll make some for everyone."

"Tilly had a hangover for two days after the last girls' night," Dad tells Daphne.

"Hey—" Daphne lifts her hands "—don't look at me. I didn't pour the alcohol down her throat."

I giggle at the memory of Tilly totally shit-faced the last time we went out. It was the drunkest I've ever seen her.

"Baby, we all have to blow off a little steam," Grandma tells Dad.

The door to the bar opens, and Marvin sticks his head in. "Am I too early?"

A few years ago, we changed the time the bar opens to one in the afternoon, but some of the regulars always try to come in early.

"Five minutes, but it's okay. Come on in, Marv," Grandma says without turning around.

"Thanks. Thanks," Marvin says.

"Well," I say, climbing off the stool. "I'm going to go open Inked. The first appointment is at two."

"I'll walk you over," Dad says, and I'm instantly on high alert.

Dad never walks me over unless there's something important he wants to talk to me about without anyone else hearing.

"Oh. Okay." I plaster a fake smile on my face.

"Uh-oh. Someone's in trouble," Daphne teases me, knowing the same thing I do.

Something's up.

"Stop it," Dad says, waving his sister off. "I want to walk my kid across the street and check out the shop."

Daphne snorts before she whispers, "Liar."

I give my grandma a quick kiss on the cheek. "See you later, Gram."

"Bye, baby doll. Love you."

"Love you too," I tell her before following my father to the door.

As soon as we're outside, he stops walking. "Why do you want to know about Wylder?"

"I told you. His kids came in, and I don't remember him from the neighborhood."

Dad raises an eyebrow. "That's it?"

I squint from the sunlight as I try to look up at him. "Yeah. That's it."

"Single father's a different ball game, Tate."

"What's that mean?"

"They're not like your usual type."

"My usual type?" I don't know if I should be offended or not. I know my dad doesn't mean anything bad by the statement.

"You have a type. Party guys. The kind that doesn't give two shits about anything or anyone. Wylder has responsibilities."

I raise my chin, feeling a little perturbed. "I'm well aware of the responsibilities of a single father."

He glances down at the cement where our shadows cross. "I just want you to put some thought into getting involved with someone like him. There're more than the two of you in the equation."

"Did you put a lot of thought into Tilly coming into our lives?"

"Of course I did, and if she hadn't been right for our family, we would've never dated."

"Do you think I'm not right for his family?"

"Baby," he says softly, his eyes back on mine. "I think you have a big heart and love deeply. Anyone would be lucky to be loved by you, including his kids. But don't get started with anything unless you're willing to go the distance. They've had enough heartbreak to last a lifetime."

"I know, Dad. We're not dating. We're not even friends. I met him once, and we had a brief conversation."

I hate lying to my father, but there is no way I want to tell him that Wylder and I kissed in a moment of weakness. I also don't want to tell him how much I liked that kiss either.

I haven't been able to get Wylder off my mind since the moment I left him standing on the sidewalk, getting a taste of his own medicine.

I'm also not going to tell my dad that I am going shopping with Wylder and his girls tomorrow. It means nothing. I am helping out a single father, but more importantly, I'll be there for his daughters to save them from the meltdown most fathers have when shopping.

"Tate," he says, lifting his hand to my face. "I love you, kiddo. I know you'll think it through before you jump in feetfirst."

"I'm not a kid anymore. I'm doing my thirties different from my twenties."

"Thank fuck," he mutters before giving me a smile. "If you do fall for Wylder, he and his kids would be lucky to have someone as sweet in their life."

"Hey, boss lady," Timber says, walking down the sidewalk toward us and saving me from the rest of the conversation. "Mr. Gallo." He tips his head toward my dad.

"Timber," Dad says before bringing his gaze back to me. "Have a good day at the shop."

"Thanks, Daddy," I say and pop up on my toes to give him a kiss on the cheek. "Good talk today, old man."

"Jerk," he mutters before he laughs.

"Come on, Timber," I say as I slink away from my dad,

never being so happy to be rescued. "We have a shop to open."

CHAPTER 9
WYLDER

"BREATHE, WYLDER," Tate says as we stand outside the dressing room at a store that only sells girl shit. Not just girl shit, but expensive girl shit.

"I'm trying," I tell her, rubbing my hands together, unable to stand still.

I hadn't realized how much the girls have grown until today. I mean, I knew Maddox was older, but I hadn't really understood the fact that she was turning into a young woman. And I hate everything about it.

Boys are next on the horizon, and the very thought makes my blood boil. I know what I was like when I was a teenager, and that terrifies me for her.

"Okay. Don't freak out," Maddox says from inside, and I turn to Tate, who looks at me with a nervous smile.

"It'll be okay," Tate whispers, touching my arm in reassurance.

"Will it, though?"

Tate nods. "They're just clothes."

Maddox walks out slowly, her face tight as she stops in front of me. "Well?"

I stare at her, soaking in the outfit and the way it fits her. There's too little cloth covering her body. Her midriff is showing, something I know will get her more attention than I'm comfortable with.

"No," I grumble, wanting to cover her with the longest, baggiest sweater.

Maddox's eyes narrow, and her face hardens. "Why?"

"I don't need to explain. It's a no."

Tate squeezes my arm. "You look beautiful, Maddy."

"Thanks, Tate," Maddy says without taking her glare off me. "At least someone likes it."

"Don't you think she looks beautiful, Wylder?" Tate asks me, trying to be the peacemaker.

I grunt. "I like it, but not on my little girl."

"Hazel's your little girl, Dad. Not me."

I grind my teeth, hating to hear the truth. I wanted to keep Maddox small, but no matter what I do, I can't stop her from growing up. Someday she'll head off to college, and I won't be able to protect her anymore.

"You can't wear that to school. It's against dress code," I say, trying to find a good reason for her not to get the outfit besides me being an asshole.

Maddy crosses her arms over her chest, and I immediately know I'm going to get pushback. "I wasn't going to wear it to school."

"Where exactly were you planning on wearing it, then?"

"When I hang out with my friends. And everything else I got today is okay for school. I want one cool outfit I can wear."

Tate's fingers tighten on my arm again, and I know she wants me to say okay, when everything inside me is screaming to say no. I take a deep breath, wanting nothing more than to see Maddy happy. That is the point of today. Something that will put a smile on their faces because they've been hurt more than I have by Katie's decision to take off.

"Okay," I whisper.

Maddy's face lights up in excitement. "Really?"

"Yeah. Why not?" I say, trying to be casual about the entire thing like I didn't just throw a fit about how little clothing covered her body.

Maddy throws herself at me, wrapping her arms around my middle like she used to when she was little. "You're the best, Dad," she mumbles into my T-shirt.

Before I have a chance to hug her back, she disentangles herself from me and takes off back into the dressing room.

"Well done," Tate says as she releases the grip on my arm.

"That was bullshit."

Tate moves in front of me and crosses her arms in the same way Maddy did. She's about to throw attitude at me. It's the universal sign to let me know I'm about to get a piece of her mind, no matter how much I don't want it. "What's bullshit?"

"You helped her railroad me into that outfit that has no business being on a girl her age."

"Wake up, Wylder. This isn't the 1800s. Women show skin."

"Women," I repeat, reminding her of the fact that

Maddy isn't a woman. She's a girl, and a young one at that.

Tate rolls her eyes and scoffs. "Don't be a prude. Maddy looked beautiful in it."

"That's the problem."

"You're going to have to come to terms with the fact that she's growing up. You can't stop it, but you can make her feel safe to come to you when shit gets hard. If you throw a man-fit every time, she's not going to tell you anything. You want to be left out in the cold?"

"Did your dad ever throw a man-fit?"

"A few times, but thank goodness Tilly was around to make sure he understood what was important."

"And that's what you're doing for me now?"

She nods. "Someone has to make you get your head out of your ass."

I jerk my head back, surprised at her sassiness, and kind of liking it too. "You have a mouth on you."

"You have no idea." She smiles.

I resist the urge to wrap my hand around that ponytail again and silence her with a kiss. "So, I'm just supposed to say nothing?"

"No. You tell her where she can and can't wear it, which you did, and leave it at that."

"And if her tits are showing?" I raise an eyebrow. This time, it was her stomach, but soon, she'll be wanting to show a lot more skin.

"How much tit are we talking?"

"Any amount of tit is too much tit."

Tate shakes her head and makes a noise. I guess she doesn't like my answer, and I already know I'm going to get an earful. "You're about to go through a lot of pain,

Wylder. You might want to invest in some stress balls or a lot of headache medicine, because I don't think you're prepared for her to get boobs."

I scrub my hand across my face and groan. "I'm not ready. Is anyone ready to see their little girl grow up?"

"I don't think you'll ever be ready, but at some point, you have to realize that you've done everything you can, and you've taught her well enough that she'll do the right thing. Did you ever teach her any self-defense?"

"No. Shit."

"We have to change that. You need to teach both girls how to defend themselves if shit goes down, because at some point in their life, it's gonna happen."

"You had shit happen to you?"

She glances away, not meeting my eyes for the first time today. "A long time ago, but yeah."

If I wasn't pissed off before, I sure as hell am now. "Who hurt you, sweetheart?" I ask without thinking, because it's none of my business.

She finally brings her gaze back to mine. "It's not important. I knew what to do, and I protected myself. You won't have to worry about how low her top is if she can break a guy's jaw or immobilize a predator."

"You're making my blood boil, Tate."

"If men weren't such shitheads, we wouldn't be having this conversation."

"Why do you think I don't want her tits showing?"

"It's not a her problem. It's a dude problem."

I repeat that statement in my head a few times as we stare at each other. She's not wrong. I haven't thought about it that way before. It doesn't matter what a woman wears or what they do. There is always an asshole out there who will hassle them.

"I'll get them enrolled in some self-defense classes after school."

Tate finally smiles again. "Good. And you'll need to practice with them too. My dad spent hours with us, teaching us what to do, until we had that shit down pat. And thank goodness he did, or else we'd be having a very different conversation."

"Will you tell me about it someday? What happened, I mean?"

She shrugs. "Maybe someday, but you're going to be even more pissed off."

"Fuck," I hiss.

Tate turns around toward the dressing room. "Hazel, baby, you okay in there?"

I've been so wrapped up in my feelings about Maddy's outfit that I didn't even realize Hazel has gone MIA.

"I'm good. I'm getting everything so far."

"Don't you want to show us, honey?" Tate calls out.

It strikes me in this moment how nice this is. Having someone else around to knock some sense into me about the girls, and life in general, is something I've missed for years. I haven't really let myself dwell on that for too long because it stirs up too many feelings about Katie's bullshit.

But even when she was around, Katie didn't talk to me like Tate does about the girls. When I look back, Katie never really gave two shits about the girls or what was best for them and us in the future.

"No."

Tate glances at me, and I shrug. Hazel's always been independent. The kid didn't even want help when she was learning to walk. She would have rather fallen flat on her behind than hold someone's hand.

"I'm going to go check on her."

"Okay," I tell her, needing a few minutes to cool off from my interaction with Maddy.

Being a dad is hard, but being a girl dad is harder, especially on my own. I want to do the best possible job for Hazel and Maddox, and I worry that I am failing and will continue to do so for years to come if I don't get my head out of my ass, like Tate said.

"Oh my goodness, you look so cute," Tate says inside the dressing room as I take a seat in the chair placed near the entrance.

"You like it?" Hazel asks her.

"Your dad is going to love it."

"Are Daddy and Maddy fighting?" Hazel asks Tate as I lean over, placing my elbows on top of my knees.

"No, baby. They're okay. They were just having a discussion."

"A loud one," Hazel says flatly.

I smile, loving my girls.

"We're not fighting. Tate set Dad straight," Maddy tells Hazel.

That statement makes me shake my head. Maddy's not wrong. She did put me in my place.

"You're the best, Tate," Hazel says.

"Yeah, she is," Maddy adds.

"You girls are too much. You're the best."

"I'm hungry," Hazel whines, and I look at my watch.

It's only been two hours since we had breakfast. I don't know how they could be hungry, but they always are.

"Me too," Maddy says.

"Where should we go for lunch?" Tate asks.

"Somewhere different. Somewhere cool," Maddy tells her.

"Chinatown?" Tate asks.

"What's that?" Hazel replies.

"I've never been there," Maddy states.

"That settles it. We're going to have the best Chinese food you've ever had."

"Yay," Hazel cheers.

"I'll be outside waiting with your dad. Take your time finishing up, and then we'll go," Tate says before she walks out of the dressing room and stops beside me. "You hear all that?"

"Yeah."

She places her small hand on my shoulder and looks down at me. "You're doing better, Wylder. I hope you like Chinese because your girls are excited."

"Are you excited?" I ask, peering up at her and itching to pull her into my lap.

"This is the best day I've had in a long time, so the answer's yes. You?"

I smile up at the woman who makes everything feel easy. "I can't remember a better one," I admit.

"There's plenty good still to come, Wylder," she tells me, smiling at me in a way that makes me believe every word of that statement.

CHAPTER 10
TATE

"WHAT'S BEAN CURD?" Hazel makes a face as she stares at the dish the waitress placed on the table. "It doesn't look good."

"It's tofu," I tell her and reach for the spoon. "It's really delicious and good for you."

I look up, catching Wylder's look of absolute disgust. "What the hell is tofu?"

"Bean curd," I say, getting a giggle out of Hazel and Maddy.

"It looks like the dirty sponge in our sink." Wylder's skin looks a bit green.

I move the spoon to his plate, depositing two decent-size pieces of fried tofu. "I promise you're going to like it. The sauce is amazing. Have I led you wrong yet?" I ask him.

His eyes move from the tofu to me, and they soften as he blows out a long breath. "No. You haven't, but I think that streak is about to be broken."

I chuckle as I offer some to Hazel. She blanches but gives me a quick nod. "You promise it tastes good?"

"I promise, sweetheart."

"I heard it's good for you, but Dad has never made it for us, and Grandma refuses to eat anything that she can't easily identify," Maddy tells me as I place a few small pieces on her plate.

"I love trying new things," I say as I get some tofu for myself.

The waitress arrives with the rest of the food, filling the table with dishes for us to share. There's fried rice, a spicy vegetable dish, egg rolls, and lo mein noodles. I didn't get too adventurous when selecting our food because I wanted to make sure the girls would eat everything, and that Wylder wouldn't lose his shit either.

"I'm more of a steak and potatoes guy," Wylder adds as he pokes the tofu with his fork.

"Shocking," I tease, giving him a playful wink. "I would've never guessed."

"I think this is neat," Hazel says as she grabs the spoon for the fried rice. "This restaurant is so cool."

"Do you come here a lot, Tate?" Maddy asks me.

"No. Usually only special occasions."

"Is this a special occasion?" Hazel asks me.

I look down at the kid. "Of course it is," I tell her, smiling back at her.

Satisfied with my answer, Hazel gives herself two generous scoops of fried rice, with only a small amount falling onto the table along the way. "What kind of egg rolls are those? Do they have shrimp in them?"

"No. They have only vegetables."

"Thank God," she says on a breath.

"You don't like seafood?"

She sticks out her tongue and gags. "No. It's gross."

"Neither of them eats it," Wylder adds.

"Me neither," I tell them, making sure the girls know they aren't alone. "I've never been able to stomach it, and the texture is weird. It's not easy being Italian because the seven fishes at Christmas is hard for me to deal with."

"Seven fishes?" Maddy asks before she jams a piece of tofu into her mouth. When she doesn't immediately spit it out, I know I have another tofu convert.

"We have seven different fish dishes on Christmas Eve. My family has had it every year since I was a little girl."

Maddy frowns. "That sounds awful."

"It is," I say.

"That sounds right up my alley," Wylder adds.

"Typical," I reply.

"That would be the worst Christmas ever."

"Well, on Christmas, we have lasagna and all those good things, but Christmas Eve is a bust."

"Ooh," Hazel croons, "I love lasagna."

"What does 'all those good things' mean?"

"What do you girls have on Christmas?" I ask them.

"Whatever Grandma and Dad make."

"Wait," I say, setting my fork on my plate to be dramatic. "Lemme guess...steak and potatoes."

Wylder nods, letting a little laugh slip. It takes me back for a second. The man has a perpetual scowl, but when he lets that mask down, he's stunning. "But I could get behind seven fishes too."

"Well, my mother's always happy to feed the masses," I say, not really thinking about how I just invited them to Christmas without a second thought.

"We could come to your house on Christmas?" Hazel says excitedly.

"Baby, we're far away from Christmas. We'll see what happens. Things change."

Hazel's little shoulders sag forward as she stabs at her tofu like she's trying to murder it. "Oh. Okay."

"Do you have any brothers or sisters?" Wylder asks, changing the subject when he realizes he's crushed Hazel's excitement.

"I do. I have two brothers, Mason and Braxton."

"I'd like to have a brother," Hazel says casually as she inspects her egg roll.

"They're not all they're cracked up to be, kid. Boys are kind of smelly." I glance up, finding Wylder staring at me. "No offense."

"None taken," he mumbles, still pushing around the tofu on his plate.

"Are they older or younger?" Maddy asks.

"Both are younger. When my dad got remarried, they had Mason, so he's much younger than me."

"So, you have a different mom?" Hazel asks.

I nod. "Yeah, but I don't think of him any differently. He's my brother, through and through."

"You think if our mom has a baby boy, they'll be our brother too?"

"Of course." But this time when I look at Wylder, he's not smiling. A mask of agitation has covered his face.

"We'll never see him anyway, so it won't matter," Maddy says without looking at anyone.

Damn.

Any happiness evaporates quickly around these kids because Katie's such a twat. I can't imagine my life without Brax and Mason, even if they are complete pains in the ass.

"They'll always be your brother," I explain, trying to take their sadness away.

"I'll make sure you see him, if that ever happens," Wylder tells the girls. "Don't worry."

Maddox peers up from her half-eaten plate of food. "You'd do that, Dad?"

"I'll always do what's best for you, and knowing your brother or sister is one of those things."

"Do you have any siblings, Wylder?" I ask.

"One sister and two brothers."

"Uncle Thumper is so much fun," Hazel says, and I glance at her with my eyebrows high.

"Uncle Thumper?" I ask in shock.

Hazel nods. "I think they call him that because he had a rabbit as a pet."

Wylder chuckles under his breath. "Something like that."

"I think I know him. Long gray beard and a tattoo of a bald eagle on his arm?" I ask because there's no way the two can be related.

Thumper is in the same MC as Rowdy. The bunch of assholes that wanted to end me not that long ago. Before then, Thumper was always nice to me, but when they thought I ratted out the club, all of them wanted to see me dead.

Wylder nods. "That's him and the one who gave me this." He points at the black eye that's now turned all different shades of purple.

I grimace. "He did that?"

"Yep. He's an asshole."

He was that. Unfortunately, I learned it when it was too late.

Hazel gasps. "Bad word, Daddy."

"I'll pay the swear jaw when I get home, princess."

"You've sworn a lot today."

Wylder glances up toward the ceiling of the restaurant. "The kid hears everything," he mutters. "I'll throw a twenty in there to cover the rest of the day. Happy, Hazel?"

Hazel nods with a giggle. "It's getting really full."

Wylder looks at me, still holding the tofu on his fork. "When the jar is full, I let the girls decide what to do with it."

"Last time, we bought a trampoline," Maddy tells me.

"Don't forget the video games," Hazel adds.

I raise an eyebrow as I look at Wylder. "I bet it fills up fast, huh?"

"Too quick," he grumbles, but I think he secretly loves it.

"What are you guys going to get next?"

Maddy shrugs. "Hazel wants a new swing set for the backyard."

"And you don't?" I ask her when she seems less than enthused about the prospect.

"I'm kind of old for swings."

"You're never too old for swings. They're relaxing. I always walk away with a clear head after I swing a while."

"You have a swing set?" Hazel asks.

I shake my head. "Not at my place, but my parents have one from when we were little."

"Lucky," Hazel whispers.

"I'm good with getting one. Maybe I'll like it," Maddy says, but only because I said I loved mine. Typical kid.

Wylder lifts his fork closer to his mouth, and all movement at the table stops.

"Are you all going to stare at me?" His eyes move around the table to the three of us.

"Yep," I snap, waiting on pins and needles to see his response.

Tofu isn't for everybody, but they make the best at this restaurant. And when it's fried in a great sauce, the texture is good, and it takes on the flavor of whatever is covering it.

He mutters quietly under his breath, but not loud enough for us to hear. Not even Hazel can make out what I assume is a string of very creative curse words.

Being Wylder, he moves the fork as slowly as he possibly can before placing it in his mouth. He starts to chew and stops, but he doesn't say a word.

"Well?" I ask.

He chews again and stops, looking down at the plate in the middle of the table.

"Anything?" I ask, trying to get an answer from him.

He swallows, but he makes it look like it was a bunch of knives sliding down his throat.

So dramatic. Typical.

"I'll tell you if I like it when you tell me how you know my brother."

"Are you in the MC with him?" I ask, wondering how I would've missed Wylder back in the day when I hung out at the compound.

Wylder thankfully shakes his head. "No. I'm not in any

club. I ride for fun, but sometimes I hang out with the guys when they're out for the night."

"Thank God," I whisper.

"How do you know him?"

"I knew a few guys in the club."

"Knew as in *knew*?"

"I was younger and dumber then."

"We all go through that period."

"Did you know my brother, as in know him?"

"What's that mean?" Hazel asks.

"Don't worry about it, baby. Eat your egg roll."

Hazel sticks out her tongue, showing the first bit of attitude before she takes a giant bite out of the vegetable egg roll.

"I met him a few times. He was always nice to me."

"Shocking," Wylder says.

"How was the tofu?"

He leans back, setting his fork down. I can't imagine what's running through his head, but I can guess it's nothing good. "It was fine, but I couldn't eat only that for a meal."

"That's why we have rice, veggies, egg rolls, and lo mein."

There was no need for me to rattle off everything on the table, but I am buying myself time before he hits me with a bunch of questions. I know they'll come. He'll have to get answers from me, or else he'll go straight to his brother and hear all about what happened years ago.

"We'll finish this conversation later," Wylder informs me like he's the boss of this conversation.

I lift my chin, filling my mouth with the biggest piece

of tofu on my plate, and give him a thumbs-up. It's the only thing I can think of to stop myself from cursing him out and having to add a stack of cash to the curse jar too.

CHAPTER 11
WYLDER

I SIT down on the porch swing next to Tate. "Sorry you were stuck with us all day."

She takes a sip of her wine, using her bare toes to push us backward. "I had a good time today. I didn't feel stuck at all."

"I know I've already said this, but they're good kids. They appreciated you hanging out with us, and I did too."

"They have a good dad, Wylder," she tells me, staring out across the front yard. "You don't give yourself enough credit. You held it together pretty well most of the day. You did better than I expected."

"I fucked up with the last outfit, huh?"

She smiles but keeps her eyes straight ahead. "Nah. It's forgotten because you let her get those clothes."

"It's that easy?"

She turns to look at me, her brown eyes meeting mine. "Sometimes."

"Are you that easy?"

She smiles and shakes her head. "We get harder as we get older."

"Great," I mutter. "Lucky me."

"Are you easier?"

"I've never been easy a day in my life."

"Shocking," she teases before taking a sip of her wine. It's not the good stuff, just an old bottle I opened a week ago when my sister dropped by for dinner.

"I want to talk about—"

"No," she says before I have a chance to finish the statement.

"No?"

"No."

"Did he hurt you?"

"Your brother?"

I nod, curling my hand into a fist. "If he did, he and I are going to have words."

"It's not your business, and it was a long time ago."

"How long ago?"

"Five years...maybe a bit more."

I slide my body over, tucking a leg underneath me so I can face her. "I know how those guys are. What happened? If you don't tell me, I'll go to my brother and find out."

She goes back to staring out across the front yard like she's deep in thought. "Can't you leave well enough alone?"

"No. I'm not built that way."

"Maybe you're defective."

"Come on, Tate. I promise not to freak out."

"I've heard that lie before. I do have two brothers and four very protective uncles."

I set down my beer and hold up two fingers on one hand and cross my heart with the other. "I swear. Scout's honor."

"Oh brother," she mutters and turns to face me, sitting the same way I am. "Fine."

I settle in, grabbing my beer again so I have something to do with my hands while she tells me the entire story. "Thank you, Tate."

"Don't thank me yet. It's not a nice story. It's long and kind of nuts."

No matter what she tells me, Thumper and I are going to have words. I want to make sure whatever it is stays in the past and doesn't become an issue for her in the future. "I'm listening."

"I met Rowdy when I was sixteen."

"Rowdy," I grumble, always having hated that loud-mouthed asshole who couldn't keep his dick in his pants for more than five minutes.

"You know him?"

"I've met him a few times and thought he was a tool."

Tate spits her wine back into her glass, almost choking with laughter. "Accurate, but when I was sixteen, I thought he was cool."

"Wait, if you were sixteen, then he was..."

"Twenty-one."

"Babe."

She lifts a hand. "I know. I know. I'm older now and realize it wasn't right or cool like I thought when I was a dumbass kid."

"Thank fuck," I mutter.

"We saw each other casually on and off for years. I knew who he was, what he was, and how he was, but I never expected anything more. We called it quits completely about a year before he was arrested."

"I heard about that when he disappeared for a while."

"Eventually, they all get caught," she admits, but anyone who has a criminal in their life knows they can't outrun the law forever. "Well, when he was arrested, the club felt there had been pressure from law enforcement."

"Okay," I say, wondering where the hell this is going to go.

"And the club thought I must've ratted them and Rowdy out to the cops, because, of course, I'm a woman, and in their mind, I had to be petty and heartbroken."

I tilt my head, surprised anyone would think Tate would go running to the cops after so many years of what I can only think would've been bullshit with Rowdy. "They thought that?"

The man always had his arm around a different woman. I don't remember ever seeing Tate when I had run into him. I'd remember her face if she had been there. It's unforgettable.

She nods slowly. "They were out to get me."

"Out to get you?" I ask, tilting my head and curling my fingers into a tight fist, imagining how terrified she had to have been.

"Yeah. I left town for a little while until shit got settled. My great-uncles in Florida stepped in and made sure the club knew it wasn't me, and until they decided to leave me alone."

"Was it that simple?"

She shakes her head and glances away for a moment before bringing her sorrowful eyes back to me. "Logger came after me. Know him?"

I nod. "Yeah, but he disappeared a while ago."

"I hope the asshole's dead."

I raise my eyebrows, surprised at her venom. "That bad?"

"Fucker had a gun on me, but luckily, my uncles showed up before he had a chance to shoot me."

"I hope he's dead too," I tell her, feeling a red-hot streak up the center of my back. My heart's racing, and an anger I haven't felt in so long takes hold. "Because if he isn't, he should be."

"Wylder." She stares at me.

"Tate." I stare back.

"Wylder, be serious."

"I am."

"You're a dad."

"And?"

"You have two sweet girls in there—" she points to the windows on the porch "—and they depend on you. You can't go off trying to rescue a woman you barely know from something that happened years ago."

"Have any of them reached out to you since?"

Tate shakes her head. "I put the MC behind me, and when I turned thirty, I promised myself I'd never date a biker again."

I learn two things from her last sentence. She's thirty, which is way younger than me, and she doesn't want to date a biker. "Bikers in a club, guys who ride bikes, or both?"

"Bikers in a club. I don't need that kind of hassle and bullshit in my life. I already have a nosy family. I don't need a nosy club too."

"I love riding my bike, but for the life of me, I could

never understand why my brother, or anyone for that matter, wants or needs to be part of a club. It's caused him nothing but trouble over his life."

"I love motorcycles too, but the MC life isn't for me. I wasn't born to be someone's old lady and turn the other cheek as they do bad shit. I want my partner to put me and our family before a bunch of leather-clad men."

"That's how it should be."

"Tate," Hazel says, running out of the house with her favorite teddy bear tucked in the crook of her arm. She's moving so fast, she almost tips over when she stops in front of Tate. "Do you want to see my room?" She doesn't wait for Tate to say yes before grabbing her hand, trying to yank her off the swing.

Tate glances at me with a nervous smile. "Is it okay?"

"Yeah, babe. It's good."

"Babe," Hazel repeats before she giggles.

I hadn't even realized I'd called her that. "Sorry."

"I've been called worse," she says as Hazel pulls her upward and then toward the screen door.

As soon as Tate and Hazel disappear inside, Maddox comes outside to join me on the porch. "How's it going?" she asks as she slides into Tate's spot on the swing.

"Good," I say, drawing out the word and wondering where the heck Maddox is about to go with this.

"I like her, Dad."

"Me too, kiddo."

"I like her for you," she explains.

I rub my palm down and up my jean-covered thigh. "It's not like that."

"It should be."

"I just met her."

"So." Maddox holds my eyes.

"It's complicated."

"Because of us?"

"No, sweetheart."

"Then how's it complicated?"

I never thought I'd be having this conversation with my kid, but here I am. And knowing Maddy, she isn't going to stop until I give her a reason. "I'm older than her."

"Someone has to be."

I sigh and shake my head. The kid always has an answer for everything.

"You're also not getting any younger either."

I'm stunned into silence, something that doesn't happen very often.

Maddox reaches over and takes my hand in hers. "Hazel and I were talking, and we think it's time you get back out there and date again. You were happier today than you've been in a very long time."

"That was because I was spending the day shopping with my girls."

Maddox tilts her head and purses her lips. "It's not nice to lie, Dad."

"Did you two set this up? Get Tate inside so you could have a talk with me?"

Maddox shrugs and smirks innocently. "Maybe," she sings.

I pull her against me and kiss the top of her head. "I love you, sweetheart. You have such a big heart."

She peers up at me with her big brown eyes. "So do you, Daddy, and you need to share it with someone other than us, and we like Tate."

I never thought my kids would like someone else in my life who wasn't their mother. Maybe I haven't given them enough credit.

"We'll see, sweetheart."

"Don't wait too long, or you'll be sorry."

Tate and Hazel come back outside, and it hits me. I like this. No. I love this. Hazel's smiling, Maddy's curled up next to me, and there's a beautiful woman, who's also one hell of a kisser, with us too. She looks like she's always been here... She belongs.

CHAPTER 12
TATE

"TATE."

I glance toward the street, finding my grandmother on the sidewalk. For a moment, I freeze, surprised to see her this far away from home.

"Gram, what are you doing down here?"

"That's your grandma?" Maddox asks, sitting on the swing next to Wylder.

"Yeah," I say softly, taking a few steps toward the railing with Hazel still holding my hand.

"She looks sweet," Hazel adds.

"I went to the specialty shop around the corner to get something for dinner tomorrow." Her eyes dip to my hand, seeing Hazel's fingers intertwined with mine. "What are you doing down here?"

"We went shopping," Hazel answers before I have a chance to.

"Fun," Gram says. "Hi, Wylder."

"Hi, Mrs. G. Would you like a glass of water or something else?" Wylder asks her from his spot next to Maddox. "You're welcome to come sit for a while."

For a moment, my heart melts from the sweetness, but a second later, I know this could be a complete disaster.

First, it's bad enough that my gram saw me here. I know it will soon be followed by a lengthy session of being questioned about everything that happened and where it could go.

Second, news will travel fast that I was on Wylder's front porch, looking a little cozy with his kids. Gram doesn't have the ability to keep secrets. No one in my family does.

"Don't mind if I do," she says.

Wylder's off the bench, and he heads toward my grandma, taking the bag from her hands. She smiles up at him as she wraps her hand around his arm for stability. "You were always a good boy, Wylder."

He chuckles as he moves her up the walkway. "You're not a good liar, Mrs. G. We both know I had my moments."

She pauses at the base of the porch stairs and peers up at him. "Honey, when you raise three boys and work in a bar like I did, I've seen more things than you could ever imagine. Your idea of good and mine might be different, but I know good when I see it. And you are, in fact, good."

"You're a good one too, Mrs. G."

I don't say anything as Wylder holds on to my grandmother as they climb the three small steps to the porch.

"Well, isn't this a beautiful spot," she says, glancing around the porch.

It is, too. I can't imagine Wylder decorated the porch on his own. It's way too pretty to be done by a man. Maybe he has a knack for design and décor that he's been hiding from everyone.

"Maddox did it all. She loves decorating and design."

Maddox is beaming. "I love it out here," she says, and I can see the pride on her face at the compliment from my grandmother and her father.

"You should, dear. You did an amazing job," my grandma says as she plops down in an empty chair.

I know I couldn't have made this front porch prettier than Maddox. She certainly has an eye for details, and her creativity is beyond anything I had at her age.

"It's impressive, Maddy," I tell her. "Maybe I can get your input on the shop. It could use some sprucing up."

"I love sprucing things up," she tells me with a big smile.

"As long as your father is okay with you helping me."

Maddox turns to her father, her eyes pleading. She is a pro at learning to control him with a single glance. If he tells her no, he's instantly going to go back on her shit list.

"Sure. On the weekends and not on school nights."

Maddox almost throws herself at her father and snakes her arms around his shoulders. "You're the best."

He touches her back, his eyes big as he stares at me in shock.

"We'll set up a time for maybe next weekend to meet, and I can show you the space."

"If you can text me the style you want, I can start making an inspiration board."

"A what?"

"It's like a gallery of ideas," she explains, and I suddenly feel stupid.

"Oh. How delightful," my grandmother says, her gaze moving around the porch to each of us.

I know my gram, and in her head, she's already planning our wedding. Every time I've brought someone around the family, she is ready to marry me off. The woman is relentless in wanting to be a great-grandmother, and since I'm the oldest, she thinks I'm going to be the first one to do it.

"You know…" She pauses and folds her hands in her lap. "Tomorrow, we're having a big dinner down at the bar. I know doing it on Monday is a bit strange, but the bar is too busy on the weekends to do it then."

Oh shit.

She's starting to put her wild ideas into action.

"We shut the bar down, and the entire family comes. We used to do it at my place, but the family's too large for that now. The bar is the next best option. You three should join us and bring Cheryl too."

"Really?" Hazel says with a squeeze of my hand.

"Every week," I say, but a little part of me is hoping Wylder says no.

Wylder and I are friends. We're only friends. Friends who shared two kisses, but still, we haven't discussed moving beyond that point. Dinner with my family is a big freaking deal.

"Are you sure?" he asks my gram, but his eyes are firmly planted on me.

"I insist," Gram says without a thought of how I'll feel or what kind of message a dinner with my family sends to Wylder—but more importantly, his kids.

"Maddy and I can bake cookies," Hazel says, trying to earn them a spot at the table.

"I'm not sure tomorrow is a good night for us."

Maddox's shoulders slump immediately.

Fuck.

"You should come," I lie to him, more for the sake of his girls than him. "It's always a good time."

"Please, Daddy." Hazel puffs out her bottom lip, laying it on real thick for the old man. She's a pro too. I wouldn't be able to say no to that face.

"As long as Tate doesn't mind."

"No. Not at all," I say, my voice cracking a bit.

"Why would Tate mind?" Gram asks. "We have friends to dinner all the time, and you two are friends, right?" She looks at me when she asks the last question.

Now she's lying. Rarely are friends invited unless it's a special occasion, which it isn't.

Betty Gallo was a pistol in her day. Hell, she still is. The woman always has something up her sleeve, and my grandfather is no better.

The two scheme something terrible. If there's a plot being hatched, they're the ones behind it. I don't know how my dad ever survived with them as parents and turned out as sweet as he is.

"We are, but we just met a few days ago, Gram."

"Well, I've known Wylder since he was little and Cheryl for over forty years. If I don't call that a friend, I don't know what is."

"Do you want us to bring cookies or something?" Wylder asks my gram.

She shakes her head, her box-dyed hair barely moving because of all the hair spray she uses. "No, honey. Tilly will bring some stuff from her bakery."

Maddox and Hazel gasp in unison, which gets them a big smile from Gram.

"Any special requests?" Gram asks them.

"Anything," Maddox answers.

"Everything," Hazel adds.

I chuckle because I feel the same.

I love my grandma's cooking, but there's something about Tilly's bakery that just does it for me. Maybe it's because it brings me back to my childhood when she'd take me to the shop and let me try everything as she baked. It was every little kid's dream.

Gram looks down at her gold wristwatch. "I better run. Tate, will you help me down the stairs, baby?" She lifts her arm and waits for me to move.

As I reach for her, I snag the bag of groceries from near her feet. "Of course, Gram. Want me to walk you home?" I hint, trying to find an easy exit because we had our shopping day together, but I think it's time for me to go.

She shakes her head as she uses me as leverage to get up. "No, baby. Stay here with your friends." When she looks at me before placing her foot on the first step, I see the devious gleam in her eyes.

I wait until we're closer to the sidewalk to say something to her. "I know what you're up to, Gram."

She pulls her head back as she looks at me. "I don't even know what you mean, sweetheart."

"Gram," I whisper to avoid the girls from overhearing the conversation. "We're barely friends. Don't get your hopes up for something more."

"Baby," she whispers back. "The look on that man's face when he glances your way has nothing to do with friendship. You need to get your head out of your cute little ass and open your eyes. Wylder's a good man, and he needs a good woman instead of that tramp of an ex-wife he had in the past and that trash biker Rowdy you spent too much time with. You two make a good match. He needs a little fun, and you need stability. It's a match made in heaven."

"You're setting yourself up for disappointment."

"We'll see," she says with a smile and raises her hand to wave to the three onlookers on the porch. "See you tomorrow evening."

"We'll be there," Wylder says.

"He has a lovely voice. I could listen to him for hours," she says to me as she grabs the bag of groceries from my hand. "Bye, sweetheart. See you tomorrow."

I stand there, watching her walk away, completely dumb struck at my grandmother's conniving. She never said much about Rowdy when I was with him, but ever since I was almost killed because of him, she hasn't held her tongue.

My grandfather never lived his life on the up-and-up, and even did a stint or two in prison, but they refer to it as college when in mixed company. They've never gone into details, but I can tell my grandmother's still pissed at him about it.

When I turn back around, the girls are leaning forward against the railing, watching my grandmother walk away.

"This is the best day ever," Hazel says as she fingers the end of her braid.

Wylder's eyes are trained on me as I climb the stairs, finding my seat next to him still open.

"I'm going to go inside to start looking at ideas for the

shop," Maddox announces. "Maybe we can talk about it more tomorrow at dinner?"

"That sounds nice," I say to her as I take a seat next to Wylder, trying to ignore the fact that he's still staring at me.

"You're the best, Tate," Maddox says before disappearing through the screen door. "Come inside, Hazel."

"I better go," Hazel says as she drags her feet across the wooden porch. "Maddy needs me."

When she disappears, Wylder says, "They're not obvious or anything."

"Neither is my gram."

He smiles at me, looking so much younger when he's happy and not brooding. "I can cancel tomorrow if you're uncomfortable. I'll make a believable excuse that won't draw any attention. No harm, no foul."

"You'd do that?"

"I'd do anything to make you happy."

My heart beats a little faster because no one besides my father has ever said those words to me.

I've always had this special talent for pushing away the good guys and being a magnet for the shitheads like Rowdy.

How can I tell Wylder not to come now?

I can't.

CHAPTER 13
WYLDER

"DO I LOOK OKAY?" Ma asks as we stand outside the Hook and Hustle entrance.

"Ma, you've been here a hundred times and know everyone inside. You look great like you always do. Don't make a big deal out of this."

She nervously pushes on her curls. "Yes, but I've never been invited to a private dinner. This is a big deal, son. I don't know anyone else who's ever been invited either."

I haven't put much thought into being asked to join them tonight. I assumed Mrs. Gallo was only being kind, but when I think about it...really think about...it's not normal for them to invite people outside the family, just like my mother said.

The door to the bar opens, and Mrs. Gallo sticks her head out. "There you guys are. We've been waiting for you."

My mother steps in front of me to hug Betty. "I'm sorry we're late. I couldn't figure out what to wear."

"We're casual, honey. You look beautiful, though," Mrs.

Gallo tells her as she hugs my mother back. "I hope you girls are hungry. We have a feast inside."

Hazel's stomach gurgles, getting a giggle out of all of us. "I've been saving room all day."

"I'm starving too," Maddy adds as we follow my mother and Mrs. Gallo toward the front door.

When we walk inside, the bar looks the same and somehow different. It's bright and brimming with the loud chatter of a room filled with people. No one's sitting at the bar nursing a cheap beer like they usually are.

The entire family is milling around, talking to one another loudly with animation. If it were anyone else, I'd think they were yelling at one another, but the amount of laughter and smiles tells me otherwise.

I've known the Gallos my entire life. It's hard not to when everyone knows everyone in this neighborhood. There are no secrets either. Gossip runs rampant around here, and I've done my best to keep my name out of everyone's mouth. I knew to hang out in other neighborhoods if I wanted to keep under the radar of most of the people my mother knew.

"Wylder," Daphne says, walking toward me with her arms outstretched. "You're looking well."

"Hey, Daphne. You do too," I tell her as she gives me a quick hug and pulls away.

When I was little, I had the biggest crush on Daphne Gallo. She was stunning, with a splash of rocker girl that sent my heart racing every time I laid eyes on her.

"I'm so glad my mom invited you guys."

"Me too," I say, but I'm not convinced accepting the invitation was the right thing to do.

We are virtually strangers. Sure, we know each other

from the neighborhood, but by no means does that warrant an invite to a family meal. But I know what is going on, and I can't say I'm not happy about it.

Tate's grandmother is doing her best to make things happen between me and Tate. I'm pretty sure she has no idea about the two kisses we exchanged inside and outside Tate's shop across the street.

"This is amazing," Hazel says at my side as she snakes her hand into mine. "Can I have one of those?" She points at a tray of cupcakes.

"Well, if it isn't one of my favorite Shirley Temple drinkers, Hazel." Daphne bends down and smiles at my little girl. "I haven't seen you in a stitch, but you've grown. Soon, you'll be as tall as your daddy."

Hazel cranes her neck back to look up at me. "I don't think I'll ever be as tall as him. He's huge."

Daphne chuckles. "I bet you'll give him a run for his money someday."

Hazel brings her gaze back to Daphne. "What's that mean?"

"Never mind. You can have as many cupcakes as your daddy says you can."

Hazel's eyes are back on me, pleading with me in the silent way she does that makes it impossible for me to say no. Girls, man. "One for now, and you can have more after dinner."

Hazel squeals and takes off toward the cupcakes a few feet away.

"She's a cutie pie."

"She's going to be trouble someday."

Daphne chuckles. "I have a feeling she already is."

"Hi," Maddox says, walking up to us. "I'm Maddox."

"Such a rock star girl name," Daphne tells her, which earns her a smile.

"I like it," Maddox says and shocks the shit out of me because I've heard her moan about how she doesn't like being different from everyone else and how she thinks it's a boy's name.

"I heard you're going to help Tate redecorate her shop."

Maddox is instantly beaming. "I am. I can't wait."

"There he is," Vinnie, Tate's uncle, says as he stalks across the room, looking as big as ever.

The man spent years playing professional football for Chicago. He's something of a local legend because of his skills on the field and for helping to finally bring a national championship to the city after decades of mediocrity.

"Vinnie," I say, holding out my hand to him.

We've talked a few times over the years. The last time I had a real conversation with him was when he came into the body shop to have his car repainted.

His grip is so tight, I almost wince, but I refuse to let him know he's crushing my fingers. "Ma told me you were coming to dinner with your girls, and I was shocked. But we're glad you're here."

"No one more shocked than me."

Vinnie looks almost the same as he did ten years ago. He's barely aged and continues to work out, keeping his muscles as toned as they ever were. "I'm thinking about buying a beat-up old-school GTO. Interested in refurbishing it for me?"

"Nice. Those are kick-ass, man. For sure. I'd be honored to work on it for you."

"Baby, come meet Wylder. He's a genius with cars," he

says to a beautiful woman who's standing only a few feet away.

Damn. There's not an ugly person in the room. If pretty comes on a gene, every person in this family has it.

"This is my wife, Bianca," he tells me, wrapping his arm around her waist.

"She's a famous writer," Ma says at my side, almost making me jump out of my boots because I didn't know she was nearby.

Bianca smiles at my mother and extends her hand to me. "I'm more known around here for being Vinnie's wife than my ability to put words on a page."

"Oh, honey," Ma says to her as I shake Bianca's hand, "Don't sell yourself short. I love football, but there's nothing better than getting lost in one of your steamy romance books."

"Thanks, Cheryl. You're always so sweet to me," Bianca says with a tip of her head.

"Wylder's going to work on that GTO for me."

"Great," Bianca mutters, not sounding the least bit enthused about the project.

"Hey," Tate says, coming to my side. "You okay?"

"Yeah, babe," I say without thinking. "All good."

Bianca, Vinnie, and Daphne raise their eyebrows for a brief moment before letting their surprise fade away.

"Want a beer?"

"No," I tell her, glancing over at the girls, who are drooling over a table filled with desserts. "I'll take a water, though."

"On it," she says before stalking away from us with a sway of her hips that has me thinking all the dirty thoughts.

"So," Vinnie says, leaning closer to me. "You two a thing?"

"We're friends."

"Mm-hm," Daphne mumbles. "Whatever you say, Wylder."

"I'm older."

"And?" Bianca asks as she leans into Vinnie.

"We barely know each other."

"She'd be good for you, and you her," Daphne replies.

"Daphne, I have a lot of baggage."

"Who doesn't, Wylder?"

I have no response. I'm shocked and stunned into silence that Tate's aunt is basically giving her blessing.

"Wylder," Angelo, Tate's dad, says as he approaches our group. "How are you?"

"Good. You?" I ask, keeping the conversation short because the last thing I want is to piss him off.

He's a big man. I know how protective I am of my girls, and I'm sure he feels the same way about Tate. I don't think my girls will ever be too old for me to worry about them and their happiness.

"I'm well. Can we talk?"

"Sure." I swallow, wishing Tate had come back with my water.

"Ohh," Daphne whispers, teasing me and getting a scowl from her brother.

"What's up?" I ask as we move a few feet away from the group.

"I don't know what's going on between you and Tate..."

"We're friends," I repeat. I think it is a statement I am going to say dozens of times before the end of the day.

"Sure," he mutters, staring me right in the eyes. "Just don't break her heart. I know you've been through some shit, and so has she. You two could use a break."

Is he giving me his blessing? For the second time, I'm stunned into silence.

"And you have two young girls to think about too. I've done the single-dad dating thing, and it's not easy. You have a lot of people's feelings to worry about in that situation, both big and small."

I nod, not sure what to say.

"Take things slow."

I blink as it finally hits me.

He is giving me his blessing.

"And if you hurt her, I'm going to hurt you."

I muster a nervous smile. "Got it."

"Good. We understand each other."

"Perfectly," I say.

"I'd hate for those to be the last two kids you ever have." He smiles sweetly, like he didn't just threaten to castrate me.

"Me too," I whisper.

"Daddy," Tate says to him as she slides in at my side. "What are you doing?"

"Talking about the neighborhood," he lies.

She narrows her eyes at him because she knows he's lying, just like my girls know when I am too. "Ma wants you in the kitchen."

"Okay," he says before starting to move. "Good to talk to you, Wylder."

"You too, Mr. Gallo."

"Angelo," he calls out, and he walks across the bar.

"What did he say?"

"Not much and nothing bad," I reassure her.

She hands me the water bottle, giving me the same look she gave her father. "You're a shit liar just like he is, Wylder."

"We were having a dad-to-dad talk."

She covers her face with her hand. "How embarrassing."

"Your family is great," I tell her, twisting off the top of my water and doing everything in my power not to touch her.

"They're something."

"I envy you," I tell her.

Although I have brothers and a sister, my parents were only children. We didn't have huge family get-togethers or weekly family dinners. It was always just us.

"For what?"

"For all of this," I say, ticking my head toward the bar filled with people she is related to.

"Sometimes they're a bit much. But you're right. I really am lucky to have them."

If I could have one wish, it would be for my kids to have a group of people like this in their lives.

"The eye's looking better," she says, but she doesn't reach up to press on it this time.

"It looks like shit."

Tate chuckles. "Has anyone asked about it?"

I shake my head. "Shockingly, no."

"This group has had more black eyes than most people I know. They probably barely even noticed."

"Maddox wanted to cover it with makeup."

Tate smiles at me and touches my arm. "That would've drawn a few comments, for sure."

"Tate! Tate!" Hazel says, running toward us and coming to a skidding stop. "Did you see the cupcakes?"

Tate crouches down and taps Hazel's nose. "They're here every week, sweetheart."

Hazel's eyes widen. "Really?"

"Yeah. What's your favorite flavor?"

"Chocolate."

"Well, if you guys come back, I'll make sure there's an entire tray of chocolate ones just for you."

"You'd do that?"

"Yes," Tate says softly and so sweetly, I could pull her into my arms and hug her for being so kind to my kids.

"You're the best," Hazel says to her, throwing herself into Tate's arms and nuzzling her face into her neck.

Tate peers up at me, and I know—this is where I'm meant to be.

Who I'm meant to be with.

"Wylder," Tate says, pulling me out of my fairy tale. "Can you help me in the back? I can't reach something on the top shelf in the storage room."

"Sure," I tell her as Hazel runs back to the tray of cupcakes.

Tate takes my hand, weaving in and out of people giving us inquisitive glances. "It won't take long," she assures me, looking back at me every few steps.

I follow her to the back of the bar, and as soon as we're in the storage room, she slams the door and then me up against it. Her lips are on mine, devouring me. The kiss is needy, making my knees go weak. I wrap my arms around her, winding her ponytail through my fingers and taking control of the situation.

I want this.

I want her.

I want it all, and I'll do everything in my power to make Tate Gallo mine forever.

CHAPTER 14
TATE

"TATE. TATE," Hazel says, her voice nearly a screech as she barrels through the front door of the shop. If this were a cartoon, she'd have smoke billowing out from her shoes as she comes to a stop. "Guess what?"

I round the reception desk as Maddy walks in with less enthusiasm, which is usually the case. Teenage malaise... it's something. "What?" I ask as I kneel in front of Hazel.

"We're going to camp," she whispers as her body shakes from excitement.

"You are?" I ask with my eyebrows raised.

Hazel nods as she bites down on her lip.

"It's bullshit," Maddy mumbles behind her younger sister.

My eyebrows don't come down as I look around Hazel to where Maddy is standing. "Why don't you tell me how you really feel?"

Maddy's arms are crossed, and the look on her face is like she's eaten the sourest candy on the planet. "I don't want to spend two months in the woods. I hate nature," she mutters through gritted teeth.

"I'm sure it's not that bad."

"They have canoes," Hazel says, touching my shoulders. "I don't know what they are, but they have them."

"It's a long boat that you row," I explain to her as I tap her cute little button nose. "I love canoeing."

"Sounds horrendous," Maddy adds as her face somehow becomes even more sour. "It's in Indiana. Who the heck wants to go to Indiana for the summer?"

I hold back my laughter at her dramatics. "Indiana is beautiful."

"I want to spend the summer here with my friends."

My heart aches a little for Maddox. I know how important time with friends is at her age, but I try to keep in mind that she's going to have the summer of her life at camp. "I went to camp when I was around your age. It was my best summer ever."

I was a little older than Maddy is now when I went, but I made amazing memories and friendships that still go on to this day.

"It'll be my worst."

Wylder walks into the shop with a box from Tilly's bakery across the street. "I got everyone's favorites," he says, holding up a cup of coffee in his other hand, which instantly puts a smile on my face.

I push myself up from the floor, touching the top of Hazel's head as I walk around her to get to my coffee and Wylder. "Thank you," I whisper to him as I take the cup from his hand.

"You can't buy me off with a cupcake anymore, Dad. I'm not a little kid," Maddox grumbles.

Wylder's forced smile tightens at his daughter's displeasure, but that's not anything new. The girl likes nothing, and her favorite pastime is complaining. "Fucking impossible," he mutters as he squeezes his eyes shut.

"Did you get me a chocolate banana?" Hazel asks, oblivious to the drama unfolding around her. "It'll be a long time before I can have another one." She takes the box from Wylder's hands before he recovers from Maddox's attitude.

"It'll be okay," I whisper to him. "It's a phase, and it'll pass."

"When?" he whispers back.

"A decade," I say and instantly bite my lips to stop the laughter from bubbling out of me.

"Fuck," he groans.

"That's two dollars, Daddy," Hazel says as she peels away the paper wrapper from around the banana cupcake, which is also one of my favorites. "And Maddy owes one."

Wylder's eyes slice to Maddy as she stares at the floor, suddenly finding something interesting.

"When do the girls leave?" I ask, changing the subject.

"In two days," Maddy replies, still not meeting her father's eyes.

"We're leaving early Monday morning. It's only two hours from the city," he explains.

"Do you want to come?" Hazel asks me.

I glance at Wylder, and he nods. "Sure, baby. I'll come with you guys. I want to see if the camp is as miserable as Maddox thinks it is."

"Oh. It will be," she says. "There are going to be so many bugs. I hope you're ready to get bitten, Hazel."

Hazel's eyes grow wide at her sister's statement. "I hate bugs." She sticks out her tongue and gags. "They're the worst."

"They're as big as softballs in Indiana," Maddy adds, trying to scare the heck out of Hazel. "I haven't even mentioned the spiders."

"Maddox," Wylder snaps, making Maddy seal her lips shut in a hurry. "The bugs are no different there than here, Hazel."

"Is that true, Tate?" she asks me for confirmation.

"It's true," I lie with the best convincing head nod I can muster.

City bugs and Indiana bugs are not the same. No one will ever be able to convince me otherwise, but I can't tell the kid that. She'd have a panic attack before she even got there.

"I'm going to miss you girls this summer," I tell them.

"You'll live," Maddy whispers. The sass is strong with her today. Unusually so. She's always snippy, but not quite this much.

Wylder sighs. "Give it two weeks, Maddy. If you hate it, I'll come and get you."

She finally looks in his direction. "Promise?"

"I promise, sweetheart."

She lets out a long, loud grunt. "Fine. I can do anything for two weeks, but if you don't come and get me, I'm going to thumb my way home."

"Oh boy," I mutter, picturing her being picked up by some creepy truck driver. "Don't do that. I'll make sure he comes to get you. I promise."

But I have a feeling after two weeks at camp and making new friends, Maddox isn't going to want to come home early. I thought I'd hate it too, but there's something exciting about being away from home, surrounded by friends, and just having fun. It's the way it should be for kids.

"I'm holding you to that," Maddy says to me.

And I have no doubt that she will. The kid forgets nothing.

"Well, we better go. I have to get the girls packed up, and the list of shit they need to bring is a mile long."

"That's three dollars," Hazel says without missing a beat.

"Want any help? I have the evening off, and Timber can close up the shop."

Wylder's shoulders relax. "That would be great. I could use a second set of hands and eyes."

"Yay!" Hazel fist-punches the air. "Tate's coming over."

"I'll bring pizza with me too."

"From the bar?" Maddy asks with a glimmer of light in her eyes for the first time since she walked into the shop.

"Of course. They have the best pizza in town."

"They really do," Maddy says. "Pepperoni and black olive, please."

"Well, duh," I say with a smile.

Wylder snakes his arm around me, and he doesn't hesitate to kiss my cheek in front of the girls. "See you tonight. You're a lifesaver."

"Anything for the girls." I love spending time with all three of them. I'd be lying if I didn't admit that I was more than a little excited to have some time alone with Wylder without the girls around, too. "And you can think of a creative way to thank me later," I whisper so only he can hear me.

We're still new. Wylder and I are still feeling each other out, trying to decide whether this is right for us and for his kids. I wouldn't even say we were a couple. We haven't spoken the words to each other yet, and no promises have been made. There's still a part of me that keeps setting off warning bells not to jump in feet-first and get ahead of myself. Wylder's been alone since Katie, the skanky ex-wife, walked away from him and the girls.

Wylder gives me a wink before he and the girls walk out of the shop without leaving me a cupcake. They're not even gone sixty seconds when Tilly walks out of her bakery and hauls ass across the street. She always looks stunning and so put-together. Even with three kids at home, she never set foot outside with a hair out of place.

Tilly meets my eyes as I watch her through the giant window at the front of my shop, and she waves.

I'm at the door when her hand touches the handle. "What's wrong?" I ask her.

She gives me a sweet smile, the same one she always has on her face. I swear she never has a bad mood. "Nothing, honey. I just talked to Wylder and heard the girls are heading out of town."

"Yeah," I draw out, confused.

"That'll make for an exciting summer for you."

My belly does a little flip. "I don't know. Maybe."

"Maybe?" She touches my cheek, and somehow her palm is cool even though it's hot as hell outside. It's a late spring heatwave. "Honey, you'll finally get some time alone. Take this from someone who dated a single father, time alone is precious, especially this early in a relationship."

I small pang of guilt washes over me. It couldn't have

been easy for her and Dad, even though we loved her from the moment she came into our lives. They never had much time alone except when my grandparents took us for a few weekends here and there. "I suppose so."

"I like Wylder. Lord knows he's better than Rowdy—but then again, almost anyone is." She chuckles as she drops her hand from my face. "I see the way you look at Wylder. You're smitten, baby."

"Smitten has gotten me in trouble in the past, Ma." I collapse into a waiting room chair and blow out a long breath. "I don't want to make that mistake again."

"We all make mistakes when it comes to love," she says as she takes the seat next to me, covering my hand with hers. "But if you find the right person, all the mistakes before them will be worth it."

"My last one almost got me killed. I'm pretty sure nothing was worth losing my life."

"Rowdy didn't lead a normal life, kid. He was surrounded by the worst kind of trouble, and you got yourself wrapped up in it too. That's not Wylder."

I lean over, placing my head to rest on her shoulder. "Were you worried about getting involved with a single dad?"

"Of course. I didn't want to fall in love with you and Brax if the relationship wasn't going to work out. But I didn't let my fear and possible heartache stop me, and I'm glad I didn't. I have three beautiful children and a husband who still makes my toes curl."

"Ma. Please."

Tilly giggles. "Although, at my age, when my toes curl, it often leads to the worst muscle cramp ever."

"Ugh," I groan.

"Anyway," she continues like she wasn't just talking about her and my dad having sex, "I think you should let your guard down and see where the summer takes you. You'll have some time without the girls around to figure out if you're the right fit."

"Two months isn't very long."

She turns to me and stares straight into my eyes. "It's long enough to know if he's your forever, baby girl."

CHAPTER 15
TATE

HAZEL WIPES at a tear that's sliding down her cheek, nearly breaking my heart. I kneel in front of her, grabbing ahold of her arms to comfort her.

"You're going to have such a good time."

"I'm going to miss you," she sniffles, looking so tiny and young among the other kids.

My heart aches in an unexpected way. She's not my kid, but that doesn't mean I feel great about leaving her.

"I'm itching already," Maddox whines as she drags a suitcase over the dirt-and-gravel path like it's filled with bricks. "This sucks."

Wylder hoists a duffel bag over his shoulder, the second piece of luggage Maddox has packed even though she claims she'll be out of here when her two-week stay is done. "Did you pack the itch cream and bug spray?" he asks her.

"Of course, Dad. Duh." Maddox rolls her eyes, but thankfully, Wylder doesn't see it because he has only the smallest shred of patience left.

Wylder mutters under his breath and shakes his head but doesn't say anything more to her.

The girls complained the entire car ride. It didn't bother me. They were just being kids and were probably nervous but had no other way to voice their worries besides whining about everything.

A woman's voice comes through the speaker, and everyone in the area looks up as if we're going to see her lurking somewhere. "Welcome, campers. Set your watches for seven o'clock. We're holding a s'mores-eating contest, and the winner will earn the premium cabin for themselves and the roommates of their choice. The cabin has air conditioning, a big-screen television, and a private bathroom. Be ready and be hungry."

"Oh. My. Goodness," Hazel exclaims with wide eyes. "All-I-can-eat s'mores?"

I nod, unable to hold back my smile at her sudden change of mood. "You're going to eat until you puke, huh, kiddo?"

Hazel giggles and twists her body back and forth like she's ready to jump out of her skin. "Maybe."

"If you win, I'm your new and only roomie," Maddox tells her, already pinning her hopes and dreams on her little sister.

Hazel glowers at her big sister with so much sass, I have to hold back my laughter. "Well, duh. It's not like I know anyone else, Maddy."

She sounds more and more like Maddox every day. She's growing up too fast, even in the short amount of time I've known her.

"I'll get Maddy settled in and come back for Hazel,"

Wylder says to me as he adjusts the duffel bag on his shoulder.

"I can handle her," I tell him, wanting to be a little useful because standing here doing nothing isn't an option.

I've already been given more than a few dirty looks from the mothers who are wandering around with their noses in the air. I don't fit in here, but that's no shocker. We're in the middle of Indiana, and I look like I stepped out of an issue of the newest tattoo magazine on the newsstand.

Wylder nods his approval. "I'll meet you at her cabin in a few."

"Sounds good," I tell him as Hazel twists around, no doubt daydreaming about chocolate and marshmallows.

Wylder and Maddox head off, leaving me with Hazel.

"Ready?" I ask her, pulling her back to the here and now with my voice.

She slides her tiny hand into mine before tipping her head back, giving me the biggest smile. "This is going to be the best summer ever."

My heart melts a little at her excitement and her hand in mine. This kid is quickly stealing my heart with her sweetness.

She deserves a good summer. Lord knows they've had enough bad shit because of their bitch mother ditching them like an old pair of shoes.

"I hope so, sweetie," I say to her as I glance around, trying to figure out where the hell I'm going.

Hazel's in cabin forty-seven, and we're standing in front of cabin six.

"This way," she says, dragging me to the right like she

knows where she's going. I follow without giving it a second thought. She's a smart kid. Observant. Maybe even a little too much for her age.

In less time than I thought, we're standing in front of her cabin. Hazel stops, turns, and stares at the wooden building like it's the most beautiful thing she's ever seen.

"This is it," she whispers, and she clutches my hand a little tighter, as if she's trying to ground herself to this very spot.

"You nervous?"

"No," she answers quickly. "I won't be here long. I'm getting the penthouse."

I chuckle at her self-confidence. "Okey dokey."

"You'll see."

I have no doubt this kid can eat a mountain of s'mores, and I also know she'll throw up by the end of the evening because she won't know when to stop. Whoever came up with the idea wasn't too bright because who wants to start camp with a bunch of sick kids? Not me.

"Will you come in with me?" she asks, giving me her big doe eyes.

"Well, duh," I say, giving her the same answer she gave to Maddy. "I would never just leave you here."

But as soon as the words are out of my mouth, I feel a burn deep in my chest. How would she know I wouldn't leave her? Her mother did.

She exhales and gives my hand a squeeze. "As Tone Loc once said, let's do it."

I stare down at her in disbelief as we take our first step toward her cabin. "How do you know Tone Loc?"

Hazel giggles. "Grandma loves him."

"Huh," I whisper, completely shocked.

"She likes to put it on and dance around the house."

I would've never pegged Cheryl as a Tone Loc fan. Not in a million years. And to think about her dancing around the house, shaking her ass, is on a whole different level. Mind blown.

The cabin door swings open before we make it onto the first step. A little girl comes barreling out, running down the steps so fast, I immediately brace for impact.

"I'm Credence," she says, wrapping her arms around Hazel and shaking with so much excitement, I'm surprised she doesn't levitate off the ground. "What's your name? We're roomies."

"Hazel." She flicks her gaze at me, looking scared.

Credence finally releases Hazel from her grip before throwing her arm around Hazel's shoulder. "We're going to have the best summer. Wait until you meet the other girls."

"The others?" Hazel asks, swallowing nervously.

"Iris and Avery. They're cool like us, though."

I smirk, wondering what makes a kid cool these days. They've known each other for a few minutes and have already come to a determination.

I follow the two girls as we head up the steps, but I almost trip when I see the most beautiful and elegant woman filling the doorframe.

"Who's this?" she asks Credence with a smile.

"Hazel. My other roomie."

"And this?" the woman says as her eyes drag up me with nothing but a look of disgust on her face.

Bitch.

"My dad's girlfriend," Hazel answers before I have a chance to say anything.

Am I his girlfriend? We haven't made any promises to each other. Not that I'd say no, but I'm still trying to hold on to the rules I set forth for myself on my last birthday.

"I'm Tate," I answer. "A friend of the family."

"And the mother?" the woman asks, glancing around like someone is going to materialize out of nowhere.

"She left us," Hazel says like it's not a big deal and totally normal, when it isn't. "But we have Tate now."

That ache from earlier is back and more painful than before. If I ever meet the bitch, I am going to knock her teeth out for what she did to Hazel and Maddox.

The woman's eyes widen. "Oh. I'm sorry," she whispers. I hope the nosy bitch chokes on her fake apology.

"It's okay. I like Tate more," Hazel replies to the woman, walking right by her as she says it.

"I made it," Wylder says as he comes up behind me. "Everything okay?"

"Yeah. I was just talking to…"

The woman doesn't hide her sneer as she says, "Camilla."

A stuck-up name for a stuck-up woman. Serendipity.

"I'm Wylder. Hazel's father."

"Credence's mother," she says, finally letting her bitch smile drop.

"I'm going to go say goodbye to Hazel, and then we can dip," he says as he brushes his hand across my back. "Okay?"

"Yeah," I say, relishing the light touch. "I'll chat with Camilla."

Wylder jogs up the steps to the cabin, giving Camilla a brief chin thrust like she's one of his buddies.

But instead of chatting, Camilla and I stare at each other, totally silent.

Thankfully, Wylder's back outside a moment later. "She's settling in. Ready?"

"Yep," I snap, still holding Camilla's gaze.

He slides his arm around my body, turning me around. "Later, Cammy," Wylder calls as we walk away.

Damn it. I wish I could've seen her face. I bet her lips were puckered up like a tight asshole from the nickname. I'm sure no one has ever called her Cammy. It's way too casual for a woman with her attitude.

"She was pleasant," Wylder says to me as he guides me down the gravel-covered path.

"You can't be serious," I mutter.

"If she was wound any tighter, she'd be a knot," he jokes, pulling me against him until our hips bump. "She reminds me of someone I know."

I bump him back. "I hope you're not talking about me."

"I meant my ex."

Camilla is exactly how I picture Katie. Neither one of them is anything like me...thank God.

"Thanks for coming with me today. It meant a lot to the girls."

I turn my head to face him. "And you?" I ask.

"You're so needy."

"That's not an answer."

He tips his head down, brushing his lips against my forehead. "And me too."

"Better," I tell him, smirking at the validation and probably neediness too. "I wanted to be here for the girls."

"And me?" he asks, being just as needy as me.

"You too." I laugh at our ridiculousness.

It's easy to be around Wylder. Too easy. Alarm bells should be going off in my head, but they're not. And that's concerning and comforting. It's a strange mix of emotions I'm not sure I can reconcile.

Rowdy and I never really did anything together unless I begged him to go somewhere with me. Rowdy was about a good time. That good time almost left me six feet underground, though. Totally not worth it. No amount of good dick is.

"What now?" I ask, suddenly feeling a little weird because we usually have to look over our shoulders for two sets of young eyes.

"Now, we have an entire summer to ourselves."

My belly does a little flip at the thought of having days, weeks, even more than one month with Wylder to myself.

"And I plan to take full advantage of it too."

"Advantage of time or me?"

Wylder leans over, bringing his mouth close to my ear. "Both," he growls.

CHAPTER 16
WYLDER

"I'M NOT A FAN," Tate says at my side as we pass by another line of trees.

"Of what?"

"This state."

I smile, watching two assholes weave in and out of traffic on this two-lane highway. "Not my favorite either."

"There's nothing interesting to look at."

"Maybe there's the world's largest ball of yarn or some shit around here."

Tate groans. "The landscape is so boring that that almost sounds good."

The truck yanks to the right, and I grip the steering wheel tighter, doing everything in my power to keep the beast under control.

"What the hell?" Tate asks, gripping the dashboard like it's somehow going to save her life if shit goes even more south.

I let off the gas, easing the truck onto the berm without

running over all the bullshit left by other vehicles that have been in the same predicament as us.

"Fuck," I hiss as the car comes to a screeching halt.

Tate's shoulders sag forward as she sucks in a breath and finally releases her grip on the dashboard. "That was almost more than my heart can handle."

"I did the best I could."

This isn't good. Whatever's wrong, I can guarantee it isn't something that's a quick fix, especially since we're in the middle of nowhere. We'd have a better chance of finding parts to fix a horse-drawn buggy than my classic Scout I just finished refurbishing.

"I'm sure you can fix it."

I turn my eyes toward her, hating that I have to kill her optimism so quickly. "Babe, brace yourself for a long wait."

"Like how long?"

"If it happens today, it'll be a goddamn miracle."

Her mouth drops open, and she blinks at me in shock. "Say that again, because I'm pretty sure I didn't hear you right."

"This isn't the type of car you grab spare parts for at the local auto store. It's a classic."

She rolls her eyes. "Of course it is, but you're a wiz with these things. It's literally your job."

"Exactly. Which is how I know this isn't going to be an easy fix."

She covers her face with her hands before she slowly drags them down her face. "Why couldn't we break down in a more interesting place? Now what?"

"Now, we call a tow and figure out our next move."

She lifts her arm and points to the sky, where the

clouds have shifted to a dark gray. "Looks like a storm is headed our way too."

"The universe likes to pile shit on."

It's not the first time I've broken down, but it's the first real crisis, if you could call it that, that Tate and I are facing together.

"I'll call a tow and figure shit out. We can either rent a car and I'll come back for the truck, or we can wait it out wherever the fuck we can lay our head tonight."

She grabs her phone from the seat and starts to type away at her screen. "You call a tow, and I'll start looking at places. There's no need to leave this old girl behind."

So far, I'd give her an A. Katie would've already started screaming about what an idiot I am for driving such an old piece of shit. Every single day, I'm reminded of all the ways they're different.

"I'm on it."

Surprisingly, roadside assistance is sending someone immediately. The chatty lady on the other end of the phone told me they were having a light day, and she didn't want Daryl to leave us stranded in the rain.

"They're on their way," I tell Tate as soon as I disconnect the call.

Her tongue is out, sweeping across her bottom lip and tempting me to haul my ass across the front seat. "I found a few places for us to hunker down for the night."

"I don't want a shit place."

"Do I look like the kind of girl who stays in shit places?" she deadpans.

"No."

"Then zip it."

"Zipped," I tell her, pinching my fingers together and dragging them across my lips.

"It's almost shocking the number of cute cabins around here."

"I like the sound of that."

"Hot tub?" she asks, one eyebrow raised.

"I'm liking it even more, but we'll have to see how far away they're taking the car before we make any final plans."

"Fingers crossed."

Lucky for us, Daryl shows up a few minutes later, looking every bit like I'd imagined he would. He has a big potbelly with his pants hanging underneath and a blue shirt barely covering him. The old baseball hat on his head is covered with grease and is no doubt nothing like the original color.

He makes quick work of hooking us up and spends the entire time talking about the Scout. He doesn't stop gushing about the restoration job.

"There's an inn near the shop," he tells us. "It's probably not as swanky as you're used to in the big city, but it's comfortable and clean."

I turn my gaze toward Tate, knowing she has her heart set on the cabin idea. "Whatever she wants to do."

Tate jams her phone into her back pocket. "The cabins require more than a one-night stay. The inn is fine."

"And that storm is fixin' to be here soon."

"We don't have a car to get out to the cabins anyway. The inn is perfectly fine."

"The storm's going to be a doozy," Daryl says as thunder booms in the distance, shaking the ground. "We'll be lucky to keep power around these parts. Not the type of night you'd want to be in a secluded cabin away from civilization. Best part, I can drop you at the inn before I drop your girl off." He pats the hood on the Scout, looking at her with so much love in his eyes.

"Thanks, Daryl. It sounds great," Tate tells him.

She's really good with everyone. I've never seen her treat someone poorly, which is something I really like about her.

On the way to the inn, Daryl tells us everything about the small town not far from the highway. He tells us about all the things to do, which isn't much to us, but to him, it's everything. It's the place he's called home since he drew his first breath.

There's a family-owned restaurant that closes at eight and serves the best pancakes in a fifty-mile radius, based on his experience. There's a shop with anything we may need for our brief stay and a sports shop where we can get gear if we want to do any fishing or other outdoor activities.

I almost chuckle when he tells us the last bit. There's nothing about Tate and me that screams outdoorsy. We don't even look like the type that would hike up a mountain—or, when talking about Indiana...all the flat land.

"Thanks, Daryl. You'd been really helpful," I tell him as he pulls in front of the inn, which is really a bed-and-breakfast in what looks like the oldest house I'd ever seen.

"Tell Elizabeth I sent you. She'll treat you real good." He gives us a toothy smile. "I'll give Marvin all your details, and he'll be in touch about the ol' girl."

"Thanks again," I tell him as I shake his hand, and Tate shimmies her way out of the front seat.

"You kids have fun, but not too much," he says with a wink.

I imagine this is the type of town where most sexual activity besides missionary is illegal. Sex is for baby-making and not fun. Total snoozefest. I thank my lucky stars every day I wasn't born in a place like this. I would've been miserable and probably drunk myself to death to dull the monotony.

"Well," Tate says as I walk up next to her. She tips her head back, glimpsing up at the old building painted a shade of gray that's almost as dark as the sky. "It's no cabin, but I think this'll do."

"It'll be whatever we make it," I tell her, wrapping an arm around her waist and pulling her close to me as a flash of lightning causes both of us to flinch.

"Fuck. We better get inside before we get drenched," she says, tugging me forward with her. "Or struck by lightning."

I follow her, not putting up a fight because there's no person I'd rather be stranded with than Tate. We've spent a lot of time together, but there's been a time limit because the girls are always around when they aren't at my mother's or at school. This is going to be our first real test of alone time without any interruptions.

No family. No kids. No nothing. Just us.

A woman is in the hallway as soon as we walk through the front door, the lightning outside sending shadows across the space as well as her face.

"Welcome to the Saybrook. I'm Elizabeth," she says with a warm smile. She looks like a grandma with big-rimmed glasses, an oversized flowery dress, and her short gray hair curled tightly around the crown of her head. "Do you two need a room?"

"Please," Tate says sweetly. "We'd love to stay the night if you have a room or two."

I almost choke on the word two and work quickly to correct the statement. "We only need one."

Elizabeth gives us a devilish smile as she laughs softly. "Of course. You're in luck because we only have one left. It's a queen bed. Is that okay?"

Thunder sounds in the distance as the windows rattle from the rain.

"It'll do perfectly," I tell her. I wouldn't care if we had a twin as long as we have a dry and warm place to spend the night alone. Sleeping won't be in the cards tonight if I have my way either.

"Excellent," Elizabeth says, moving to a small desk near the stairway. "It has a private bath and a very large tub." The last statement, she says with a wink pointed in our direction.

"I could use a good soak," Tate tells her, reaching into her purse.

I push her hand down before reaching for my wallet. "I got this."

"Dinner's in an hour, or I can bring it up to your room and leave it outside your door."

"Outside the door would be great," I tell her as I give her my credit card for the night.

"I figured you kids would want to settle in and relax."

"Daryl told us this place is the best in town," Tate adds, remembering that Daryl told us to mention him to Elizabeth. Maybe he gets a kickback.

She waves her hand in the air and laughs. "We're the only place in town. Daryl's such a character."

"That he is," I say as I take back my credit card when she hands it to me.

"He's my brother-in-law. One of the nicest guys in town, though. My sister couldn't have done any better."

Again, I couldn't do small town. The very thought makes me want to jump out of my skin.

She hands me a key with a giant white feather dangling from the keychain. "Top floor. Complete privacy. It's the only room up there, but beware, the floors are thin," she says before biting her lip like she's reading my thoughts.

"We'll be quiet."

"No one said you had to be. Just letting you know you may have an audience if you get too loud." She winks at me.

Tate giggles softly behind me. "If we're too much, just give us a holler," she tells Elizabeth. "It's our first night without the kids."

I glance over my shoulder at Tate. She made us sound like a couple, something I want more than I think I've ever expressed to her.

Tate gives me the same wink Elizabeth just gave me, but hers is much more sinful.

"Oh dear. That calls for a celebration. I'll add a bottle of wine on the house to go with your dinner."

Tate turns her attention back toward Elizabeth. "You're the best, Elizabeth."

"Call me Liz."

"Liz," Tate repeats. "I'm Tate and this is Wylder, but you already know that from his credit card."

"It's lovely to meet such a beautiful and young couple. We don't get many around here."

I glance around, noticing we're the youngest people in the place by decades. We sure don't look like anyone else either. If there were a picture next to "stuffy" in the dictionary, it would be of this group.

"You're too sweet," Tate replies as I shift on my feet, ready to get the small talk over with and head to the seclusion of our room. "Thanks for everything, Elizabeth. I'm going to get this grumpy fella up to his room so he can wash up for dinner."

"Of course. Of course," Elizabeth says, shooing us toward the stairway. "Enjoy yourself."

"I plan on it," I tell her with a wicked smirk.

"One more thing," Tate says, and I growl under my breath, but she just shushes me with a pat on the arm. "Are there robes in the room? We didn't bring anything to change into since we were only supposed to be gone for a few hours."

"There's two in the closet near the bathroom. They're extra soft and freshly laundered."

"Excellent," Tate breathes as her boot finally touches the first step.

I do everything in my power not to push her upward, making her move faster. If I didn't know any better, I'd say she's stalling on purpose to drive me crazy.

"Small talk's over, princess," I tell her, touching her denim-covered ass.

She shoots me a look over her shoulder, which only solidifies my thinking. She is stalling. "I'm moving, aren't I, Mr. Grumpy? You in a hurry for a shower?" she asks, pushing back on my hand as I try to propel her forward faster than her snail's pace.

"I'm in a hurry to get you naked," I tell her, quickly shutting her up.

CHAPTER 17
TATE

ELIZABETH WASN'T LYING. The bathtub is enormous and deep. This may not be a cabin with a hot tub, but it's better than I could've imagined.

"Are you coming in?" I ask Wylder as he walks into the bathroom in nothing except his jeans. His feet are bare, along with everything else. My mouth instantly waters at the sight of him. "It's warm."

Wylder's eyes drop to my body, which is concealed by perfectly placed bubbles. "Is it as hot as the sun?"

I throw my head back and giggle. "How did you know?"

"Women, man," he mutters, shaking his head as his fingers move to the button on his jeans.

"Don't be a baby. It's perfect."

"I'll be sweating in five minutes."

I laugh again. "Go slower," I tell him as he starts to undo his fly. "I want to enjoy this."

He raises an eyebrow at me as he slows his pace. "You want me to do a striptease?"

"You're basically naked already, so..." I can't tear my gaze away from his body. I could stare at him forever and never get bored. The artwork alone could take days and days of exploration.

"You want a picture?" he teases, and I drag my gaze away from his bare skin to look him in the eye.

I reach over the side of the tub to where my clothes are in a pile with my phone on top. "Well, if you're offering."

His movement stills. "Are you serious?"

"Dead," I tell him, lifting the phone in front of me and lining up the shot of his bare torso. "I needed a new screen saver."

"I get one too," he says, but I shake my head.

"With bubbles, but you're not putting my bare chest on your screen."

"That doesn't sound fair," he says before his fingers move away from his fly.

"Sucks," I tease him, snapping another photo as he starts to move the material of his jeans down his hips. "Fuck, that's hot." I stare at the photo, wanting to take another one, but I'm already pushing the bounds with the two I already took.

"I'm going to get you back," he promises.

I lick my lips, praying it's something hot. A spank on the ass would be a nice touch. I like a little pain with my pleasure, but we haven't had that conversation yet. I've fantasized about his hands around my neck more times than I even want to admit. The man does it for me.

"Put the phone down," he orders with a no-nonsense look. One I've seen before from my dad, but Wylder's isn't even half as frightening. "Picture time is over."

"Or what? Are you going to punish me?" My voice

comes out huskier than I intend, betraying my excitement at the possibility.

He shakes his head with a smirk, his pants only partially down his hips, so his dick is still tucked inside the denim. "You're trouble," he mutters.

"Only the best kind." I smile at him, tossing my phone back onto the pile of my clothes. "But what kind of punishment are we talking about if I took one more?"

We've made out a lot. Like *a lot*, a lot. The girls cut into our ability to do much else, and I told myself I'd take it slow with this man. Something I was never very good at doing in the past.

And we've done that. Lots of kissing. Lots of touching. Oral had been beyond fantastic, but skin-to-skin, knocking boots...the possibility hadn't been in the cards until now.

I am officially going to break the promises I made to myself for my thirtieth birthday. But who am I kidding? Those were pipe dreams I never had any chance of achieving unless I was going to enter the convent and become completely celibate.

He stares at me with a heated gaze, making my heart beat a little faster. "What kind do you want?"

"Take off your pants and I'll tell you."

He closes the distance between us and reaches out, touching my chin. "You do it."

I gaze up at him, licking my lips. "Me?"

He runs his thumb back and forth near my bottom lip. "Take out my cock and wrap those pretty lips around me."

My body almost trembles with need at the tone of his voice and the look in his eyes. I'm so full of lust, I almost forget to breathe.

And like a greedy little slut, I instantly move my wet

fingers to his jeans, yanking the denim down his hips. His cock springs out, waving around like it's celebrating freedom.

I wrap my fingers around the shaft, pumping a few times as he moans. I lick my lips as I bring the head of his cock closer. "You want this?" I ask as I notice Wylder's gaze darkening.

"Princess," he breathes as he places his hand on my head, guiding my mouth to his bare flesh.

I hum my approval as the silky skin slides between my lips and across my tongue. There's power in this. The way he moans and his body twitches with every movement. I am in control, and he is eating up every tantalizing second.

But before I can get comfortable, he slides his hands underneath my arms. His cock pops out of my mouth as I'm lifted in the air. "I need to be inside you," he says, his voice gravelly and full of need.

I wrap my wet legs around his body, my core to his cock, as he carries me across the small bathroom. I don't protest as he places my bare ass on the cold stone of the bathroom countertop.

We've had the sex talk. I am on birth control and have been since I turned sixteen. We are both clean and tested regularly, although neither of us has had sex with anyone else in ages.

"Fuck me," I beg, digging my heels into his ass.

Thankfully, I don't have to ask twice.

Wylder fists his cock, lining it up with my opening. His lips crash down on mine, taking my moan as he pushes himself inside at a slower pace than I expect.

He curls his hand around my neck, holding me still as

he pumps into me. My ass slides against the slippery surface, my body dripping from the bath.

The world around us falls away, and nothing or no one is as important as this moment.

Wylder wraps an arm around me, pulling my bottom closer to the edge. I lean into his embrace, giving him better access to me. He groans into my mouth as he sinks himself fully inside me.

There's nothing frantic about this. We're savoring the feel of each other, getting lost in the pleasure, until my toes curl and my body tightens.

I moan through the orgasm that grips my body as Wylder's movements become more hurried and forceful. A second later, he follows me over the cliff to ecstasy.

CHAPTER 18
WYLDER

"THAT WAS..." Tate's sleepy voice trails off as her fingernails trail tiny circles across my chest.

I grab her hand, bringing her fingers to my mouth before putting them back down. "Yeah, princess. It was."

I'm not sure I have words to describe the entire day, especially everything that has happened since we arrived at the Saybrook.

"Now what?"

"Now, we sleep."

She tips her head back and opens her eyes. "I mean about getting home."

I blow out a breath because none of the options are optimal. "We can wait here for days, we can rent a car and come back another day, or I can call my brother to bring me the part I have back at the garage to fix her."

"Which brother?" she asks.

"The dickhead."

Her fingers stop moving. "Thumper?"

I can hear the hesitation in her voice. She hates him,

and I can't blame her. The MC made her life a living hell, and if they had their way, she'd be another missing persons case that would eventually go cold.

I don't even know why I brought him up. He and I have a contentious relationship at best. "We can rent a car," I offer, not wanting her to have to make the decision.

"No. No. Do I have to be around him for long? What are we talking about here?"

"He'd drop the part and go."

"So, technically, I wouldn't necessarily have to see him at all?"

"Not if you didn't want to."

She props herself up on one elbow, staring down at me. "Have him bring the part. It makes the most sense. If he's your brother, I'll have to face him sometime. He's part of your package."

"He doesn't have to be." I've written other people off for less. The fucker should've been dead to me years ago, but I tried not to hold a grudge because my mother would be beside herself.

"He's your brother, Wylder."

"And?"

"He'll always be part of your life."

"He's an asshole, Tate."

"Well aware of that fact," she reminds me like I forgot all the bullshit she went through with the MC.

I still don't have the entire story, but I am going to change that. Thumper and I are going to have an in-depth conversation about Tate. So far, I've avoided him since we had our fight, which was the night I ended up inside Inked with my lips pressed against Tate's.

"But," she says softly, grazing my nipple with her

fingernail, "he's our best chance of getting out of here without having to come back until the girls are done with camp. I can stomach him for a few minutes if it gets us home sooner."

I stare up at her, chewing the inside of my lip. I wish there were another way, but of course, we had to break down in the middle of nowhere. "I'll make the call. I'll have you home by late tomorrow afternoon."

"Perfect," she breathes and collapses back into my side. "I have to get the guest spot ready. My cousin's coming in from Florida to do a stint at Inked. I want everything to be perfect."

"I'm sure it will be," I tell her as I grab my phone off the nightstand and find Thumper's number.

The phone rings three times and then kicks over to voice mail, which is full. But before I can shoot off a text to him, Thumper's photo flashes on my screen.

"Yo," he says before I have a chance to say hello.

"Hey."

"What's up, dickhead? You never call. You dying? Ma dead?" he rattles off. "Hopefully not Ma, but the other shit…"

"What are you doing in the morning?"

"Not a goddamn thing besides turning the bitch out who currently has her lips locked around my cock." There's a choked moan in the background, and I cringe, glancing down at Tate, who doesn't seem fazed in the slightest.

"Can you swing by my garage and drive a part out to me? I'm in Indiana."

"What the fuck are you doing there?"

"Took the girls to summer camp. The truck shit out on

me, and of course, there're no parts for it anywhere near here."

"I got you. How far?"

"Three hours."

"I'll be there by noon. Good?"

"I'll text you what I need, where it is, and where I am."

"Later," he says, the girl squealing in the background before the line disconnects.

"You didn't mention me."

"I want to have the *you* conversation when we're eye to eye. Not over the phone."

"The *me* conversation?"

I brush my lips against her hair and close my eyes. "I'm going to lay down some ground rules."

She flattens her palm against my chest and nuzzles deeper into my side. "I don't want there to be trouble because of me."

"There won't be. Lemme handle my brother. I have decades of experience with him."

"You do, but I also have a past with him. One I'd rather not repeat."

"I got you, princess. Leave my brother to me."

"Oh boy," she mutters against my skin. "This isn't going to be good."

I pull away, pushing her onto her side and curling my body against her. "Sleep. You let me worry about tomorrow."

"Okay," she says on a yawn. "He's your brother."

That is a fact I can't escape, no matter how much I wish I could. He and I have never had a good relationship. It's like he's been gunning for me since the day I was born. If there is a way to fuck me over, he does it and seems to take pleasure in it too. I am used to his bullshit, but I'm not going to let his sourness bleed onto my girl.

Which brings up another point, something she and I are going to have to talk about soon. Our relationship has been casual. It's been whatever it is. We haven't had much of a discussion about anything more serious. We've been easing into things, but that time is over.

With the girls gone for the summer, I plan to stake my claim and make her realize exactly who she belongs to—she is meant to be mine. I've never been so sure about anything in my life, and nothing is going to stop me from making that a reality.

"Sweet dreams, Wylder."

I pull her tighter against me and press my lips to the back of her shoulder. "You too, princess."

I drift off to the possibilities of a future I didn't think was possible until I met her.

———

I feel like I'm being punked as I glance around the small but full dining room. "I didn't think this shit was real."

Tate giggles across the table from me as she tears apart an everything bagel that has more cream cheese on it than should be legal. "Which part?"

I glance around, waving my hands in all directions. "All of it."

Her eyes follow the movement of my hands as she lifts a chunk of bagel to her lips. "It's nothing I've ever experienced before."

"I thought it was all made up for television. I feel like

I'm stuck in some creepy horror film and someone with a chainsaw is going to burst through the front door."

"Or that everyone's been taken over by body snatchers," she says before shoving the bite into her mouth and licking her fingers afterward.

My gaze snags on the way her lips curl around her fingertips, her tongue swiping across the smaller bits she didn't catch on the first pass. "Tate."

"Yeah?" she asks, looking at me with big doe eyes, like she doesn't know exactly what she's doing.

"If you don't stop that, I'm not going to be able to stop myself from bending you over this table and giving everyone a show."

Her smile is immediate. "They're already staring. May as well give them a good reason."

"They're staring?" I ask, clueless.

She nods. "I swear, you're oblivious to so many things."

"Why are they staring?"

She looks at me like I'm an idiot for asking such a question. "Are you serious?"

Yep. Idiot vibes. "Yeah, princess. I don't ask questions I already know the answer to."

She ticks her chin toward me as her eyes move across my exposed arms. "All of our decorations are causing a stir."

"Ridiculous," I mutter.

"Do you think anyone here has a hidden tattoo?"

I look around the room, taking in all the flannel and perfectly pressed blouses. "Nope."

"Me either," she whispers before shoving another hunk of bagel between her lips.

My phone buzzes on the table, and I glance down, seeing Thumper's message. "He's a few minutes out."

"Great," she mumbles, looking just as happy as I am to see my brother.

"At least we'll be back in the city soon and away from this." I tip my head toward the other guests. "We're not small-town people."

"I could never live anywhere except the city. I woke up in the middle of the night and lay there. You know what I heard?"

"What?" I ask before taking another sip of the too-weak coffee.

"Absolutely nothing. I thought for a minute that I maybe died, but then you moved and I knew I was still alive. It's way too quiet around here. I don't know how people sleep. They should offer white noise machines in each room."

"Only you would think it's too quiet."

"Well, you started snoring, and I immediately fell back to sleep."

"I don't snore."

She leans forward, touching my cheek. "Baby, I hate to be the one to break it to you, but you do."

"Liar," I whisper, playfully nipping at her fingertips like I am going to bite them.

She giggles but doesn't argue back as my phone pings again.

"He's here."

CHAPTER 19
TATE

THUMPER LOOKS EXACTLY like he did the last time I saw him—like an asshole. He isn't a bad-looking guy. I'm sure the ladies who hang out at the club are all too willing to spread their legs for him.

But his attitude makes him ugly. The man is full of himself. He thinks he's the creator's gift to the world.

Bleh.

He lifts a leg, climbing off the back of his bike like he's the hulk. "I made record time," he says without making eye contact with me.

Had Wylder told him about me? He has to know we are dabbling in some sort of relationship, right? I mean, no one in my family does anything without everyone knowing. I can't imagine word doesn't spread from Cheryl's lips like wildfire.

Thumper moves to the back of the bike and reaches into a leather bag he has hooked to the side. Just as he sticks his hand inside, he turns his head and his eyes land on me.

At first, he doesn't say anything. I don't either.

I stand as still as possible with my eyes narrowed. I won't show any fear. Although, the last time I laid eyes on him, I wasn't sure I'd ever draw another breath. Maybe if I don't move, I'll blend into the background somehow.

"What the..." he starts, and I know my plan didn't work.

Duh.

"Don't start," Wylder warns, his body visibly becoming rigid as he moves himself in front of me.

But I, being the nosy bitch I am and unable to back down from anything, including a fight, take one step to the left.

Thumper's eyes narrow into little slits like he's stalking prey as he steps away from the bike but doesn't pull out the much-needed part. "Brother, is that Tate, or am I seeing shit?"

"Don't make me kick your ass for a second time in as many months. I don't have the energy this morning."

Thumper lets out a loud, long chuckle. "I'm sober, and the other time, I wasn't. You couldn't knock me on my ass when my body isn't swaying."

Wylder crosses his arms, his body still tight and every muscle bulging. "Wanna bet?"

"I don't feel like riding back with bruised ribs." Thumper swipes his hand through the air, waving his brother off. "It's not worth it. You can fuck whoever you want to fuck, but," he says, raising his hand and pointing a meaty finger at me, "I'd watch out for that one."

Oh boy.

Wylder takes a step forward, the veins on the side of his neck popping out.

"Wylder," I say, reaching out to touch his arm, but he moves too far away and stalks right up to Thumper.

As soon as they're eye to eye, my heart starts to race double time. Nothing about this is good. While I'm certain Wylder would win in a fight, I don't want to watch the two of them beat each other over me.

"It's fine, Wylder. Let Thumper think what he wants," I say as they snarl at each other. I fully expect them to start foaming at the mouth with all the noises coming from them. "It's not worth it."

"Yeah, Wylder. Listen to the woman," Thumper taunts with a shitty smirk.

"*My* woman," Wylder states with a firmness to his voice that has my knees going weak.

Thumper takes a step back, his eyes roaming from Wylder to me and back to Wylder. "*Your* woman?" he asks with a raised eyebrow, looking as shocked as I feel.

We still haven't had a talk about what we are to each other. I'm not sure we're at that *mine* and *yours* part of the relationship yet.

In all honesty, I'm not even mad about it either. We're beyond the age where we need to have "the talk" to define what we are to each other…right?

Wylder closes the space between them again, and all I can do is watch as panic climbs up my throat, replacing the momentary flutter of the previous statement. "I know what happened in the past, and if you talk shit about her or come near her, I'll end you."

Thumper jerks his chin back, and his lips flatten. "You're serious?"

"Dead," Wylder grits out between his clenched teeth.

Thumper's eyes swing to me. I can almost see the

wheels turning in his brain. This is either going to go extremely bad, or we'll leave the past in the past. I don't know if Thumper has the ability to leave shit behind us. Hell, I'm not sure I have that ability either.

"She is a hot piece of ass, though," Thumper says, but his face isn't relaxed as he says it. It's like it's painful for him to admit anything positive about me, even if it is an asshole statement to make about your brother's girlfriend in front of her.

Am I pretty? I guess. I'm not ugly. I don't have a third eyeball, and I spend many a weekend waxing off the mustache on my upper lip because the Italian genes are way too strong in my family for me not to have unsightly hair somewhere.

I have a nice ass. Big and round. The perfect amount to be more than a handful for any man, even one with big hands like Wylder.

I am soft and curvy everywhere. Bones don't stick out anywhere they shouldn't. I look like one of those women in the old Renaissance paintings with lush breasts and a soft middle. I am meant for the snuggle life and to bear children because my hips are not narrow.

"Thumper," Wylder grinds out in warning.

He lifts his hands to Wylder and moves another step back. "I was paying her a compliment. I meant no harm."

"I know how you feel about women, brother. Would you say that shit if your nieces were here?"

Thumper shakes his head, looking remorseful for a second, before he drags his hand through his hair and blows out a breath. "I'm trying here, man. So much shit went down with her and Row—"

"I know," Wylder interrupts, finally releasing one of his

fists and relaxing his fingers with a few wiggles down their length. "She was innocent, and you fucked up. You almost ended her life over nothing."

Thumper grunts before responding. "We make mistakes sometimes. Shit happens."

Shit happens? Mistakes? A mistake is putting on a pink top with brown pants. A mistake is not ending an innocent person's life...my life.

"Say you're sorry."

My eyes widen. This should be good. Men like Thumper never apologize. It is damn near impossible for them to admit they are wrong about anything, and he just did that.

"You really like this girl, don't you?" Thumper asks, the reality of the situation...of us...finally making its way into his dense brain.

"I do, and so do the girls."

Thumper grumbles under his breath as his top lip curls. "Fuck."

"Mom loves her too."

If the nail wasn't secure in the coffin yet, Wylder just gave it one final whack.

"Fuckin' great," Thumper mutters.

"Say you're sorry," Wylder demands.

"For what?" Thumper asks, being an asshole.

"I don't need a fake and forced apology," I say as I take a few steps forward and wrap my fingers around Wylder's bicep. "It won't change what happened."

Wylder peers down at me, his eyes burning with anger, but I know none of it is pointed at me. "Princess, the man at least owes you an I'm sorry. You almost died."

"I remember," I tell him, brushing my fingers against

his skin to try to calm the situation. "But I'm still here and breathing. Let it go."

"Listen to the woman. I drove hours to do you a favor, and you're hassling me about bullshit that happened years ago."

"It was more than bullshit," Wylder corrects him, and I can see this is going nowhere fast.

I have to step in and do something to get this shit moving, or we'll be here all day while these two have a virtual pissing match. "Let's save the talk for another day. We're wasting time, Wylder. We need to get back to the city since I have to work this evening. Let Thumper give you the part, fix your baby, and let's dip. The other shit can wait."

Wylder blows out a long breath as a growl rumbles deep in his chest. "Fine," he bites out. "But we're going to have it eventually."

Thumper mutters some stuff under his breath as he stalks toward the back of his bike to grab the part. I stay at Wylder's side, continuing to keep a grip on his arm so we can get through the next few minutes without another incident. The sooner we get this interaction over with, the sooner we can be on our way back to civilization.

When Thumper hands Wylder the part, he says, "You want me to take her back with me?"

I study his face, trying to figure out if he's kidding. He's not laughing or smiling. He's serious, which is crazy as hell. Why in the world would he think I'd go anywhere with him or that Wylder would let him take me?

"Fuckin' no," Wylder tells him. "She's not leaving my sight, and she's definitely not going anywhere with you."

Thumper snarls at the response. "I wouldn't hurt her. She's your girl."

Wylder barks out a loud, bitter laugh. "I'll never trust you, brother."

"Your loss," Thumper says as he throws a leg over his bike and starts her up. "Someday you'll take that big stick out of your ass and figure out I'm not your enemy."

Before Wylder can reply, Thumper guns the engine and takes off.

"Asshole," Wylder whispers.

I shrug. "I've met worse."

Wylder only shakes his head in response.

"Need my help?"

"No, princess. Go inside and wait. I'll work as fast as I can, but it'll probably be an hour or so."

"Go inside and do what? Compare cross-stitching patterns with the old ladies? I'm going to walk around and see if there are any shops. Text me when you're ready."

"Don't get into too much trouble," he says as he leans over to kiss my lips, the tension from moments ago vanishing.

I snake my arms around Wylder's neck, rubbing my nose against his with a smirk. "Baby, you're the only one causing trouble around here. I'm an angel."

Wylder lets out a chuckle as his one free hand finds my ass. "You were an angel last night."

"I remember you moaning something about God."

He gives my ass cheek a rough squeeze. "It was a heavenly experience."

I drop my arms and give him a playful push. "Go, or we'll be stuck here another night. No more touching my ass until we're back in the city."

He doesn't argue with me. I know he wants out of this small-town hell just as much as I do. "I'll be quick."

"No worries," I say as my phone vibrates against my ass. When I pull the phone out of my pocket and glance down, it's exactly who I thought it would be. "Hey, baby brother."

"I really wish you'd stop calling me a baby," Brax says, his voice a little saltier than usual.

"Well, you're younger, and I didn't call you a baby. I said you were *my* baby brother, which you are."

"I tower over you."

I roll my eyes even though he can't see me. "You're right. You're big. You're bad. You're the master of the universe. Happy?"

He grunts his displeasure with my attitude. "It's a start."

"What do you want, Brax?"

"Where the hell are you? I stopped by the shop, and you weren't there."

I stroll down the sidewalk of the small town, if you can even call it that. It's minuscule. The entire downtown area could fit in half a block in my neighborhood. "I went with Wylder to take the girls to summer camp, and we broke down in the middle of nowhere."

"Sucks."

"We'll be out of here in an hour or so, though. I'm killing some time while he fixes the truck."

"Cool. Cool."

"Why'd you stop by the shop?" Sometimes getting information out of Brax, even when he's the one who initiates the conversation, is like pulling teeth.

"I needed your opinion."

"Well, you got me now. Shoot."

I hear rustling in the background on his end. "I think I'm ready to settle down."

I almost trip over my own feet as soon as the words leave his mouth. "Wait, what? I think we have a bad connection."

He groans. "You heard me just fine."

"What in the world has gotten into you, Brax? Do you even know what you're saying?"

"I'm getting bored with the games, Tate. Dating isn't fun like it used to be."

"Well, you do go through the ladies like water vanishes in a drought."

"Why do you always say weird shit?"

I chuckle as I stare at my reflection in the storefront window of a clothing store. "Am I wrong, though?"

He exhales loudly. "No."

"Maybe try to get to know a woman before you sleep with her. You might not go through them as quickly as you have been. Are there even any women left in Chicago you haven't slept with?"

"Come on. I'm not that bad."

"You are, brother. What's your thing with relationships? Have you ever had a steady girlfriend?"

I cycle through all the women who have come and gone over the last ten years. Not one of them stuck around longer than a month or two. I didn't even bother learning their names because I knew they weren't going to be there long.

"Amber."

"Who?"

"Long red hair."

"Ah. I remember her," I lie because he's been with more than one redhead, and I'm not about to waste time trying to figure out which one she was. "How long was that?"

"A little over a month."

"I hate to break it to you, but a month isn't a long-term relationship."

"I know. It's like I have a block. I don't know what it is."

I know what it is, and so does he. We don't talk about Mom often, but we saw the heartbreak my dad went through when she died. We were little, but the memories of that time are burned into our brains.

"Maybe you just haven't found the right one. When you do, you'll know it and won't want her to get away after a month."

"You think?"

"Yeah, and maybe get off those dating apps and stop hooking up with the women at the bar."

He sighs. "You sure are killing all my fun."

"You asked for my opinion. I'm giving it, but that doesn't mean you have to listen to me."

"Did you know it?"

"Know what?"

"Did you know it with Wylder?"

"Did I know what with Wylder?"

"Jesus, Tate. Keep up. Did you know you didn't want him to get away as soon as you met him?"

Flashbacks of the moment I met him when I walked the girls home after they snuck out flash through my head. He was a grumpy bastard but hot as sin, and I wanted to climb him like a tree.

"No, but he's growing on me."

"So, someone has to grow on me?"

I chuckle. "No, silly. I've been burned too many times, and my shield is a little bit thicker than yours. Wylder and I met under strange circumstances. I'd say the second time I met him, he made my toes curl, and I'm not sure there was any turning back after that."

"So, you're officially a thing?" he asks.

"I think so," I whisper, pacing in front of the clothing shop. "We haven't really talked about what we are, but I think so."

"Ridiculous. Why is shit this complicated?"

"Because love isn't always easy."

He gasps. "Do you love him?"

My stomach flips at the question. "I have feelings for him, but love... It's too early."

"Could you love him?"

"Yes," I breathe.

"I like that for you. He's a good dude."

"Yeah. I haven't found anything I dislike about him."

"That's big, coming from you."

"It kind of is."

"Where do you think I should look for someone?"

"Don't look. She'll find you when you least expect it. I know Wylder did."

"I got to run," Brax says. "I'm meeting my buddies at the gym. Maybe I'll stop by the shop later."

"You should. Our cousins get in this evening. Drop by and see them."

"I forgot about that. I'll drop by for sure."

"Later, baby brother," I say, teasing him.

"Bye, asshole," he says with a chuckle before the call disconnects.

I glance back up, staring through the glass to see the most beautiful silk and lace nightgown against the wall of the store. I want it. It would be a great reminder of this trip and make the perfect surprise for the next night Wylder and I spend together.

The door to the store isn't even fully open when a woman appears, greeting me and ushering me inside.

"Hi," I say back, feeling a little uncomfortable at how quickly she descended on me. At the stores closer to home, I practically have to hunt down a salesperson to buy something, but not here. Some people would find it refreshing, but I am too used to my space.

"What can I help you with today?"

I point to the nightgown, soaking in its beauty.

"Ah," she says with a cluck of her tongue. "It's a stunning little number."

"I want it."

"Do you want to know the price?"

"Doesn't matter. It's coming home with me."

"For a special someone in your life?"

"Yes," I tell her.

She gives me a wink. "I'll get that wrapped up for you. It's going to look stunning on you."

"I'm hoping it doesn't stay on too long, if you know what I mean," I say, giving her a wink back.

She chuckles as she moves toward the nightgown and takes it down from the wall. "If the man has any sense and has eyes, it won't last long, sweetie."

I am ending the road trip with a souvenir and a new

boyfriend. It's amazing how quickly things change, but I am ready for it, hoping shit won't go sideways when we get back to reality.

CHAPTER 20
WYLDER

"WHAT ARE YOU DOING LATER?" Tate asks as I stop the truck in front of Inked.

"Nothing."

"Come back here."

"When?"

"After nine."

"That's late."

"The night is just getting started then, Gramps."

"Hey now," I say, reaching out to grab her hand. "I don't think you were calling me gramps last night."

She smiles at me as her cheeks pinken. "Is it past your bedtime?"

"No."

"I want you to meet my cousins. You're going to love them. We can grab a beer with them, and then maybe…"

"Maybe what?"

She leans across the bench seat and brushes her lips against mine. "Then we'll see what you deserve." Her eyes sparkle with so much mischief that my cock is instantly at attention.

"I'll be here."

She slides her hand against my legs, nearly touching my dick. "I'm sure you will." And before I can pull her in and give her a deep kiss, she slides across the seat and climbs out.

"That's it?" I ask, staring at her in disbelief.

"If you want more, you'll be here."

"Don't worry. I'm coming."

"If you're lucky," she says with a wink before closing the truck door.

"Tease!" I yell out to her as she stalks toward her shop door with her hips swaying, giving me the best show.

"You love it," she calls out.

I sit there for a moment, watching her as she unlocks the door. I don't pull away until she walks inside and flips on the lights. All I can do is shake my head. The girl is impossible, and I love that about her. She's not easy, and she sure as hell keeps me on my toes.

Before I have a chance to pull away from the curb, I get a text.

Ma: Can you drop by? My sink is leaking.

It's like she has ESP and knows exactly when I'm nearby.

Me: On my way.

There is no need to waste time and put off fixing her sink. I have a few hours to kill, and since the girls aren't waiting for me, I have more free time on my hands than I know what to do with.

Ma is waiting for me on her front porch when I pull up.

She is sitting on the top step, coffee cup in hand, staring out across the neighborhood.

"How was your first night without the girls?" Ma asks as I stride up the walkway to her house.

"Interesting."

She sits a little straighter. "Do tell."

I grab her coffee cup from her hands and take a sip as I sit down next to her. "We broke down partway back."

"Oh dear," she whispers, snatching the mug from my grip. "There's a fresh pot inside."

I give her a smile, loving my ma. She's never liked to share, especially her coffee. Then there is the germ thing. Even though we are her children, she's always claimed we are dirtier than most people solely because we're boys.

"Your cup is always better."

"Two spoons of sugar and a splash of cream. It's not magic, baby."

"It's always more delicious when you make it."

She groans and hands her coffee over to me. "I'll make a fresh cup."

I knew she'd give it over. Not because she doesn't want me to make my own, but because I already took a sip and she doesn't want my cooties. I love my ma, but she is a bit of a germaphobe and has been as far back as I can remember.

"Were you stuck in the truck all night?"

"No. We found a B&B nearby, and Thumper brought me the part this morning."

"You should really get a newer car. Something that you can easily get the parts for when you need them."

"Ma."

"Vintage doesn't mean better. You need something reliable. And that old thing—" she points at the black Scout "—is not." She bumps me with her shoulder. "So..."

"So," I say before taking another sip of the coffee.

"How was your night?"

I turn my head, finding her hopeful expression. "Ma."

"What?" she asks innocently. "Did you get separate rooms?"

I shake my head. "They only had one room."

"Ooh," she coos. "How romantic."

I groan into the mug, hating talking to my mother about these things, but she always wants to know everything.

"First, let's talk about your brother driving all the way out there for you, and then we're going to get to the good stuff."

I flatten my boots out on the bottom step and rest my elbows on my knees, bracing myself. "Thumper was Thumper."

"But he brought you the part?"

"Yeah."

"I guess he's not always an asshole."

I stare at her, waiting for her to come to her senses.

"An asshole wouldn't have driven hours to bring you a part, baby."

"Sometimes, and I mean very rarely, he has a moment where he's normal, before his asshole side comes roaring back."

"Well, I'm glad he could help."

"He started talking shit about Tate."

Her mouth drops open. "Fuck."

"Yep."

"Why would he do that?"

"She has a past with the club. It's too much to explain, but he was rude, and I made sure he knew I wasn't about to let that slide."

"Did he apologize?"

I bark out a laugh. "Does he ever?"

My brother is a lot of things, but sorry for anything he's ever done wrong to me or those around him...never.

"I'll speak to him."

"Don't." I lean over, stretching my back after such a long ride. "Either he does or he doesn't, but I want it to be on him and not because his mom made him do it."

She places her hand on my back, rubbing gently like she used to when I was little. "Okay, baby. I'm sure he'll come to his senses."

I peer over at her.

"It could happen."

"I'm not holding my breath."

"You really like her, huh?"

"I do, Ma. I'm all twisted up over her, and I don't know how I feel about that. I swore I'd never—"

"Don't let that bitch Katie ruin everything for you. Not all women are careless, heartless jerks like her. I've known Tate since she was a little girl. She's a good one, and her family is the best too. No one better than the Gallos."

"It's hard to trust."

"I've never known her to be a liar."

"No, Ma. I mean to trust myself. I thought Katie loved me. I thought she was something that she wasn't."

"She was a chameleon, that one. I never liked her, but I bit my tongue because you were into her."

"Don't hold your tongue ever again."

"But how you got two beautiful and sweet girls out of such a monster is beyond me."

"I wouldn't change a thing, Ma. Without my time with Katie, I wouldn't have Hazel and Maddox."

"Sometimes the best things come out of a flaming pile of crap."

I snort at her statement. "You're so eloquent."

"Well, tell me I'm wrong."

"You're not."

"So, baby, you and Tate officially a thing now?"

"I think so."

Ma rolls her eyes. "What the hell does that mean?"

"We didn't really talk about our status, but I kind of made some claims in front of Thumper."

"Claims?"

"I said she was mine."

Ma smiles so damn big, I'm surprised she is able to keep her eyes open. "I like that. But, son, you need to talk to her about it. You don't get to make relationship decisions without the other person agreeing to whatever it is or isn't."

"He pissed me off."

"You're a Romeo," she teases.

"It was shitty. I knew it when the words came out of my mouth, but he pissed me off so much, I couldn't stop myself."

"Men," she breathes.

"I'll talk with her."

"Good, sweetheart. Don't fuck it up."

I bark out a laugh. "Ma."

"When are you seeing her again?"

"Tonight."

"You better have the talk—and fast. Don't leave the girl hanging any longer than you already have."

"Yes, Ma."

"Now, come inside and look at the sink and tell me about how the girls did when you dropped them off at camp. I want to hear everything."

"Okay," I tell her as we push ourselves up from the step. "But there's not much to tell."

"I want to hear everything that happened yesterday." She holds open the front door for me, waiting for me to go in first. "And don't leave anything out," she says.

In no time, I have my head buried under the sink and every pipe taken apart. The pipes are old, probably older than me, and really needed to be replaced entirely, but Ma refuses.

"Just get it where there's no water dripping. We'll think about doing more later."

It's always later with her.

"Ma," a voice calls out, and my blood instantly burns hot. "I'm here."

I dislodge myself from underneath the sink and glare up at her.

She only smiles at me as she calls out to Thumper. "We're back here, baby."

"What did you do?" I whisper, trying not to raise my voice at my mother.

She's playing dirty, but I should've known better. The woman has never played fair a day in her life.

"Zip it," she tells me.

"What is this bullshit," Thumper asks as he stalks into the kitchen with as much rage in his voice as I feel in my body.

"Watch your mouth, Dante," Ma says to him like he's a little boy.

My brother may be a big bad biker in his normal life, but when Ma's around, he turns into a big old softy.

"Ma, I told you to stop calling me that."

My mother places her hands on her hips and gets as close to him as she can, but she's a good foot shorter than him. She cranes her neck to look up at his eyes. "It's your name. I gave it to you, therefore I'm going to use it. Thumper's a stupid name."

I bite my lips to hold in my laughter.

"No one calls me Dante. It's..."

"Beautiful," she finishes his statement.

"I don't look like a Dante. It's a prissy name."

"It's a handsome name for a handsome man."

"I look like a Thumper."

"You're not a rabbit," she sasses. I'm damn sure she's the only one in his life who talks to him like this, and there's not a damn thing he can do about it either.

"Why am I here, Ma? It looks like Wylder has shit handled." He doesn't look my way as he speaks. We said enough earlier today to last us a few weeks.

"What's your problem with Tate?" she asks him point-blank, being more confrontational than she's been in a long time.

He jerks his head back in shock. "What does it matter?"

Her gaze dips to me. "Your brother has a chance at happiness with a nice girl, and you're going to mess it up."

"How am I involved? I don't care who he dips his wick in."

"You be nice to that girl," she says, poking him in the chest the entire time.

I haven't moved from my spot on the kitchen floor. It's like my ass is stuck to the ceramic tile.

"I like her for him, and I don't want you to be your usual boneheaded self and mess things up for your brother. You've done enough damage to this family, and I've had it. You either act right or stop coming around, stirring up trouble for people who've done nothing to you except love you. Got it?"

He gawks at her like he's at a loss for words.

"And not only that, your nieces love her too. You may not care about anyone else's feelings, but I know how you feel about those two girls. You chase Tate away, and you're going to crush their little hearts. Do you want that shit on your conscience? They've been through enough with Katie. They don't need you causing more heartbreak."

"Okay, Ma. I got it," he whispers. "Geez."

"You do whatever you need to do to make shit right with her."

"I don't have a problem with Tate."

"Liar," I mutter, earning myself a glare from my brother.

"Some shit went down with her and the club."

Ma glares up at Thumper. "What kind of shit?"

"They wanted her dead for something she didn't do, but somehow he's still holding it against her."

Ma gasps, covering her mouth quickly with her hand. "What in the ever-loving fuck, Dante? I didn't raise you to be this way."

My brother looks like my mother's slapped him across the face.

"Leave her alone. I mean it, Dante Allen."

"Ooh," I teased because she pulled out the middle

name. If we didn't know how serious she was before, that seals the deal. Cheryl means business.

"Fucking hell," he mutters, shaking his head. "I'll steer clear. It'll be better for everyone. Happy?"

Ma shakes her head, her hands solidly back on her hips. "You'll make things right because you can't steer clear forever, especially if she becomes part of this family."

"You getting married?"

"No," I tell him as I rub my forehead.

Cheryl has really gone off the deep end with this conversation, but far be it for me to stop her.

"Just be nice," she repeats to him.

"Fine, Ma. I'll play nice," he says, hissing out the last word.

But I know my brother. No amount of my mother's intimidation is going to work. But I couldn't care less. He can pretend she doesn't exist, and I'll be okay with it. As long as he keeps his shitty comments to himself—or else we are going to have a big problem and not one I'll shy away from either.

"And you." She rounds on me. "Talk to her, and don't mess this up. Make sure you're clear what you want. Don't let Katie ruin any more things in your life. She's already taken enough."

"Got it," I tell her, knowing she's right. Tonight is the night I make Tate Gallo officially mine.

CHAPTER 21
TATE

"TATE," Gigi squeals as she comes barreling through the front door of the shop with Pike behind her. "I've missed you."

She sucks me up into an almost suffocating hug, but I don't fight it. I've missed my cousin. Over the last handful of years, as I was developing the concept for the Chicago branch of Inked, I spent a lot of time in Florida and the most time with Gigi and Lily.

While I love my cousins here in Chicago, my Florida cousins are closer to me in age. We have more in common, which makes getting along easier. And if I'm honest, I look up to my cousin Gigi. She has her shit together and has everything I want in her own personal and professional life.

"Look at you," she says, pulling back and letting her gaze rake over me. "As hot as ever."

"Thanks, cousin. You're a sight for sore eyes."

"What's this?" she asks, moving my hair away from

the side of my neck. Her eyes immediately narrow. "Is that a…"

My stomach drops, and I move my hand to the very spot she's inspecting. Wylder didn't. He wouldn't. Would he?

"You have a hickey," she breathes, and indeed, Wylder did, and he would. She gives me a little shove on the shoulder. "Good for you, girl. I hope he's hot as fuck."

"Primo," Timber says as he strolls by and lifts his fingertips to his lips, kissing their tips. "Chef's kiss."

Gigi giggles at Timber's ridiculousness. "I hope I get to meet him."

"He'll be here tonight."

"Excellent," she says as Pike drops a duffel that must weigh a ton based on the loud thump as it lands on the tile.

"Hey, Tater Tot," Pike says as he moves in to kiss my cheek. "We've missed you. You should come down and visit us this winter. Soak up a little sunshine and shit. Everyone would like to see you."

"Maybe I will do that."

I love the Florida side of the family. Part of me wishes they lived here and that we would've grown up together. I can't imagine the amount of fun and trouble we would've gotten into. Maybe that's why the branches live so far apart—they know it would be disastrous.

"Are you ready for this week?" I ask them. "This is a new experience, and you're both booked almost completely full. I made sure to leave a little wiggle room here and there."

"That's great news. I'm stoked for this week."

Dad stalks into Inked with two suitcases, one in each

hand, as they try to roll in different directions at the same time. Somehow, he maintains control of them both and looks effortless doing it, too.

"Hey, Daddy," I say, giving him my sweetest smile because he deserves nothing less.

"Kiddo." He smiles back with so much kindness.

He's set the bar. I refuse to accept anything less than the amount of love he shows me and Tilly. I want it all. The entire package. So far, Wylder's come pretty damn close, but only time will tell if we're just in the honeymoon period where he's the best version of himself. We'll see if the mask slips sometime soon, revealing an entirely different person hiding underneath.

"Let me help you, Ang," Pike says, taking a suitcase from my father's hand, along with the heavy duffel. "You wanna show me where we're staying?"

"I'll take him," Dad says before I have a chance to reply.

My father spent countless hours helping me remodel the upstairs so it would be comfortable when family visited. It was a win-win for the entire family. Even if they weren't doing a guest spot at Inked, they'd have somewhere to stay so none of our lives would have to be disrupted.

Our homes here aren't like our family's in Florida. They have huge houses, which are closer to mansions than our small Southside dwellings. They have spare bedrooms, something that is an expensive and unnecessary luxury for people living in the city.

"The shop looks better in person than in photos. You did damn good, girl," Gigi says as she turns around, soaking in the design. "You really did do copy-paste with a little twist."

"I had to go edgier."

"Hell yeah. And it fuckin' rocks too."

"Thanks for doing this," I tell her.

"I was chomping at the bit to get here."

"I mean everything, Gigi. Without your backing for this shop as a branch of Inked, I don't know if it would've been as big of a success as it has been so far."

"Are you kidding me? The idea was brilliant. I'm just pissed I didn't come up with it myself. And everybody is excited to have their turn to come up here to do a spot and visit the family." She stops in front of a black-and-white I took last time I was in Florida. It's of the outside of her shop, with palm trees illuminated by the setting sun. "This is so pretty."

"I had to have a piece of the original here."

"I'd like a copy of this for our shop. And if you could take something similar of this location, I'd like a copy of that, too, to hang with it."

I can't wipe the stupid smile off my face. "I'd be honored."

"You have a great eye. You should've been a photographer."

"You think?"

"The lighting is spectacular in this one," she says, pointing to the palm trees in the photo. I waited hours for just the right light and took so many variations to find the perfect one. "If you don't make it in tattoos, you can with a camera."

"My tattoo skills are still just average, but I want to be part of this shop as more than just the owner."

"Maybe piercing is your thing. Lily could maybe show you a thing or two when she's up here next month. Talk it over with her. She wasn't into drawing and art, but she's good with a needle. I think she secretly gets pleasure out of stabbing people."

I don't know why, but I burst into a fit of giggles thinking about my bookworm, shy cousin randomly stabbing people with a wicked smile on her face. I could one hundred percent see her finding immense joy in someone else's pain.

"She's a sadist, but she'll never admit it. No one would ever believe me either because she looks like she shits rainbows."

I laugh harder, and my eyes start to water, probably ruining my makeup, but I don't care. Gigi's cracking me up with how she's talking about Lily.

The door pops open, and my brother strolls in like he owns the place and not me. "Cousin," he calls out, moving to pick her right up off the floor like she's a yard ornament.

She smacks at his arms, but it's no use. My brother is bigger than her. She may as well be swatting a fly when her small hands land against his big biceps. "You big oaf. Put me down," she hisses, but she's smiling at him when she says it.

"You love me," he teases her, not releasing her either. "Say it, and I'll let you down."

"You're an idiot," she says, rolling her eyes.

"Say it." He smiles down at her, and it's easy to see the family resemblance. There's a look to the Gallos. The men are born big, like they've been bred that way for centuries, deep in the mountains of Italy.

"Fine," she whispers, sagging into his hold. "I love you."

The words aren't said with enthusiasm, but they're enough for my brother because he sets Gigi back down on her feet. "You look good, li'l cousin."

"You do too," she says, punching him in the arm with as much force as I think she can muster, but he doesn't move an inch. "You probably have all the women wrapped around your little wicked pinkie."

"I'm over that scene," he announces.

"Hitting for the other team now?" she asks with her head tilted and her eyes wide.

"No. I'm not playing the field anymore. I want to get serious and settle down."

Now it's Gigi's turn to burst into a fit of giggles. "Oh. Okay," she says between bouts of laughter. "That'll be fun."

"It'll be something," I add with a chuckle.

"Don't laugh at me," he says, getting testy. "I'm being serious."

"I think you've blown through every single, pretty woman within twenty miles and are out of options," I say to him without an ounce of judgment. "But I have all the faith in the world that you can find someone who will want a relationship with you."

The women have never been an issue. They've been trying to tie him down since he was a teenager, but he'd always found a reason why they'd never move on past a few dates. He is his own worst enemy when it comes to love.

"I'm not that bad," he argues.

I stare at him with zero emotion on my face. We both know he's lying, and I can wait it out until he admits it.

"You're a Gallo," Gigi says. "You are *that* bad. It's genetic."

Brax snorts a laugh. "I'm different."

"No, you're not. But when you do find the one, just like the other men in this family, you're going to love hard and deep," she explains to him as she holds his shoulder.

"I'm ready."

She smiles at him with so much love. "You say that now, but it'll knock you right on your ass."

He rubs his hands together, excited and hopeful for the future. I know my brother. He's an optimist. He can find the silver lining in anything. The guy is the epitome of turning lemons into lemonade.

"I need a change."

"A change?" Dad asks as he walks back into the lobby of the shop, with Pike right behind him.

"I'm ready to settle down," Brax tells him.

My father staggers backward, holding his chest. "Am I dying?"

"You better not be," I say, shaking my head.

I can't fathom losing my father, and it's the one thing I don't like joking about. It hits too close to home because we already lost one parent. I know it'll happen someday, but I'm not ready for it. I'm too young. He needs to be a grandpa first. I want my kids to have solid memories of my daddy and not just photographs and stories of him.

Dad drops his hand and laughs. "It's still tickin'. Don't worry, baby girl."

"It's not funny, Dad."

"So, when are you getting married and who's the lucky lady?" he asks Brax.

Brax shrugs both shoulders. "Don't know, but I'm on the hunt."

"It doesn't work that way, son. Women aren't prey. It'll happen when it happens. I wasn't expecting to meet someone, and then Tilly showed up. End of story."

"I want a woman like Tilly," he says.

I glance up at the ceiling and sigh. "Do you want a servant?"

Brax jerks his chin back, frowning. "Is that what you think Tilly is?"

"No. Tilly's the best person I know besides Dad. She's a sweetheart."

"Exactly. I want a nice girl, and if she can bake cupcakes, it's an added bonus."

My dad wraps an arm around my brother and pulls him against his side. "You're a bonehead, but I love you."

Brax peers up at our father, looking every bit like the younger version of him. "You know I'm you, right?"

Dad smiles down at him. "I know it. Lord help us all because one is enough."

"Hey," Brax says, giving Pike his normal chin-lift greeting.

"Good to see you," Pike says back, giving him the same stunted chin tick.

Men.

"It's beautiful up there, Tate. You guys did a great job."

I can't wipe the stupid smile off my face at his compliment. "Thank you. I couldn't have done it without my dad's help."

"I've got to get back to the bar. It's my night to work.

Catch you all later," my brother says, peeling himself out of my father's hold. Before he dips, he gives Gigi a kiss on the cheek. "I missed you."

"Missed you too, knucklehead," she says to him as he stalks toward the exit. "We'll be over later for a beer."

"Excellent," he says before he walks out the door and jogs across the street.

"I need to freshen up and unpack," Gigi says as she tucks herself up against her husband.

"Wylder will be here around nine, and then maybe we can head over for some drinks and food," I tell her. "Sound good?"

"Is Wylder hickey guy?" she asks, raising an eyebrow.

My father starts to cough.

"Yes," I tell her with a glare.

She laughs her ass off as she and Pike leave my father and me in the waiting room.

"Well, it could be worse," he says, finally stopping his imaginary coughing fit. "At least it's only a hickey."

I roll my eyes. "It's not even that. She's only stirring the pot."

"She's good at that."

"You can say that again. My poor cousin with three girls filled with attitude. I don't know how he survived their teen years with any form of sanity," dad says.

"You sure couldn't tell by looking at him. Uncle Joe's still got it. Man is handsome as all get-out. He has a huge social media following when he posts at the shop."

"Really?" he asks, his forehead wrinkled.

"Yeah. It's crazy. Older women are bananas. And the number of young women who have a thing for the silver fox, as they call him, is astounding."

Dad smiles. "We age like fine wine."

"Yeah," I mutter. "Unlike us. We wither away with chin hair and more lip hair than ever, but you guys only get better."

"Don't be silly, baby. You get more beautiful every single day. Just like your mom."

I'm hit by a sudden pang of sadness. "She was beautiful."

"Inside and out. I didn't deserve someone as pretty and good as her."

"Dad, you deserve only the best, and Tilly's everything I could've ever wanted if it couldn't have Mom. Mom's been gone for so long, I sometimes have a hard time remembering small details about her time with us. My memory is filled with Tilly and her love. You did well. The best."

Dad pulls me into a hug, and I melt against him as he presses his lips into my hair. "It was bumpy at times, but I'm beyond blessed. And out of everything, your mom gave me two amazing kids and another with Tilly." He pauses as I hug him tighter, pressing my cheek against his chest. "Well, at least you. Brax is still a work in progress."

I giggle against his T-shirt. "He's a pain in the ass."

"Most men are until they're like forty."

"That's no lie, Daddy."

"Speaking of which…"

I peer up at him, my arms still wrapped around his body.

"Things good with Wylder?"

"Yeah. We broke down on our way back yesterday, but Wylder fixed the Scout, and we were able to get back a few hours ago."

"It's handy when you have a man who knows a thing or two," he tells me as I step out of his embrace.

"It is. He was surprisingly calm too."

"That's what I like to hear, baby. No one has time for a mantrum."

"Mantrum?" I ask, chuckling.

"You know the type."

I nod. "I know it way too well."

"I'm glad Wylder is solid. I figured he was. Single dads raising kids on their own usually are. There's no time to worry about yourself when you have to keep two kids alive and happy."

"I'm sorry," I tell him as I realize that was his life, but he was dealing with the grief of losing his wife on top of Brax and me. He didn't have anger to propel him through things, but sadness that weighed him down.

"Don't be. I don't know if I would've survived the heartbreak without you two kids. You kept me going and gave me more joy than anything in the world during that time and after."

I pop up on my toes and press a kiss to my dad's cheek. "You're the best, Pop. I love you."

"Love you too, sweetheart. Now, I better get home before Tilly has a fit. She's cooking dinner, and I don't like to be late. It's movie night."

"I miss those," I tell him. "Give her a kiss from me."

"I will. She'll be in tomorrow with some pastries for the shop and Gigi and Pike. She wants to spoil them a little."

I smile, giving him a wave. "They'll be happy."

"Bye, baby."

"Bye, Daddy."

As soon as he's out the door, Timber comes stalking

into the waiting area. "I'm so fucking jealous. It's like a lovefest out here. I got no one, but you guys... You're a freaking army of little Italians who shower kisses and hugs on one another. It's maddening at times, but I'd give my freaking left arm for a sliver of the magic you got."

I run up to him, giving him the same hug I gave my dad. "You're my people too, Tim. We can adopt you."

"You're a silly thing. I'm a little old for adoption."

"Who says?"

When he pulls away from my hug, he's at least smiling. "Maybe I'll marry into the family."

"There's a problem with that, honey. Everyone's too young for you other than me and Brax. He's looking to settle down, but I don't think he'd dig what you have going on in your pants."

"I'd make that boy see stars," he says and laughs. "Well, just know you're lucky as fuck."

I don't need to say anything else. I know I am, and I never want to forget it.

CHAPTER 22
WYLDER

"SO, WYLDER," Gigi says from across the table, "What's your story?"

She's direct for a little thing and reminds me of Tate. Looking at them side by side, I'd assume Gigi was Tate's older sister.

"Darlin', leave the guy be," her husband says to her with his arm slung around the back of her chair and a beer in his other hand. "Don't grill the man."

"I don't mind," I tell him.

Tate snuggles into my side and peers up at me. "You seriously don't have to answer."

I give my girl a smile. "I don't have any secrets."

"Okay," she mutters, "but Gigi is super nosy."

I laugh because everyone in her family is. I've known them forever in some capacity, and all of them know everything there is to know about me. That's how it is when you grow up in this area. Everybody knows everyone.

And I've quickly learned how her family is with one

another. They hold nothing back. There's no judgment, though. When you fuck up, they're going to bust your balls, but there's no malice in it.

"Not much to tell. I'm a mechanic, divorced, and have two daughters I take care of on my own because my ex-wife moved across the country with her new, rich husband."

"You sound bitter," Gigi states, which isn't too far off the truth.

"I'm bitter for my girls. They didn't deserve what she did to them," I explain truthfully. "I wasn't surprised when Katie didn't want to stay married to me anymore, but how she did it...sucked."

Gigi nods like she understands, but I don't think anyone could unless they've been in my shoes or my girls'. "How's raising two girls on your own?"

"It's something," I mumble as I lift my beer to my lips.

Tate laughs. "They try his patience a lot. You know how we girls do," she tells Gigi. "But they're good kids."

"I love that, and I love him for you," she says, raising her eyebrows as she lifts her chin in my direction. "You weren't lying about him either."

"You talkin' about me, princess?" I ask Tate.

"I didn't have a choice since you left a mark on me." She stares up at me as she points to the spot on her neck that I had forgotten about.

"That was a mistake."

"Was it?" She raises an eyebrow.

"I got carried away."

"Ah," Gigi sighs, "New love. It's the best. So much passion. I remember when this guy," she says as she nuzzles her head against Pike's neck, "and I met. It was hot and heavy."

"It was a fling, darlin'. Spring break madness before you left me without your number. Poof. Gone. Vanished without a trace."

"But you found me. You can't stop destiny, baby," she says to him.

He grunts. "I got lucky."

"In more ways than one." She winks at him with a playful smile.

"Look at this. Nothing makes my heart happier," Mrs. Gallo says from behind me, nearly scaring the ever-loving shit out of me.

"Hey, Auntie Betty," Gigi says, pushing back her seat and standing to round the table. "Looking as good as ever."

Betty places her hand on my shoulder to steady herself. "You're a good liar, kid, but not a great one. I'm looking like a worn piece of leather and feel like I've been left out in the sun for years to wither away to nothingness."

Gigi walks over to my side to hug Betty. "You're always so dramatic and descriptive."

"It's the Gallo way, baby," Betty says as she moves her hand away from me to wrap an arm around Gigi. "I'm sure your grandpa has taught you all well."

"Of course. Of course," Gigi says as she stares down at the old woman who still sports a thick head of red hair. "Sit with us. Have a drink."

"You kids look like you're having too much fun and don't need an old woman intruding."

"Gram, come on. One drink," Tate begs.

"Would you boys mind?" she asks, looking between Pike and me.

"Never," I say, peering up at her from my seat.

"We'd be honored, auntie. Sit. Sit," Pike tells her, motioning toward the chair next to him.

She lifts her hand, waving a few fingers. "Just one beer," she says as she drops into the empty seat. "I need to get to bed. Morning comes too early at my age."

"What's new?" Gigi asks Betty as she sits back down next to Pike.

Betty leans back, shifting to find a comfortable spot on the wooden chair. "Not much. My girl has found herself a good man for once."

All eyes move to me. I'm the good man? I'm not shit, but I don't know if I'd call myself a good man. I've done things most would never dream of. I've had my moments of stupidity and carelessness. The me now, the dad, he is a good guy, but I don't know if that wipes away a past riddled with sin.

"Grandma, you're embarrassing me," Tate whispers, covering her eyes with her hand. "Wylder and I..."

This is my shot. It is time to make it clear to Tate, even though everyone else around us already seems to know.

"We're still new, but I'm the luckiest bastard in the world to have caught the eye of the most beautiful woman in the world," I tell them. "I'm honored that she's mine."

Tate's mouth opens and closes a few times as she blinks at me. "I'm yours?" I ask softly.

I lean over, cupping her chin in my palm as I gaze into her eyes. "You good with that, princess?"

She nods, her eyes still big as they stare back at me.

"Yeah," she breathes softly, as if she says the words any louder, the promise would disappear.

"See," Betty says, "a good one."

"We need a bottle of champagne to celebrate," Gigi says, but I haven't torn my eyes away from Tate.

"Is there any occasion that's not champagne-worthy, darlin'?" Pike asks her.

"Yoo-hoo," Betty says, waving her hands off to the side. "Come back to us."

Tate blinks and shakes her head like she's coming out of a trance. "Sorry," she says to her grandma before breaking eye contact with me.

"I thought you two were about to consummate the relationship right here," Betty adds.

I chuckle to myself as I lean back in my chair and reach for my beer. Betty's the original wild one of the group. There's no doubt in my mind she was a hellcat in her younger years, because even at her age now, she's a pistol.

"Grandma," Tate says with a gasp.

Betty laughs as she pats her granddaughter's hand. "I mean, I wouldn't blame you, sweetie. The man could even bring my dead ovaries back to life."

Tate shakes her head as her cheeks turn the brightest shade of pink.

Gigi snorts out a laugh. "This family is too wild sometimes. I'm the luckiest bitch in the world to have been born into it."

"Is your grandma like this?" Tate asks Gigi.

Gigi nods, dabbing the corner of her eye. "I don't know which one is worse. They're almost carbon copies, but Aunt Fran is the worst by a long shot."

"Uncle Bear seems to keep her on a tight leash," Tate replies.

Gigi nods. "He has to, because she's out of control sometimes."

Brax sets a bottle of champagne down on the table, along with five flutes he carried by the stems in his other hand. "What are we celebrating?"

Betty motions toward me and Tate. "They're officially a couple."

"I got shit to do." Brax rolls his eyes and grumbles under his breath before he stalks back toward the bar.

"What's his problem?" Betty asks as she reaches for the bottle of champagne.

"He suddenly wants to be in a committed relationship," Tate explains as she passes out the flutes.

Betty's eyes cut to Tate. "What?"

Tate nods. "I don't know what's going on with him."

"It's about damn time he stopped playing so many games. He's getting a little long in the tooth to be out there trying to repopulate the world on his own."

"Gram, you're on fire tonight," Tate says to her.

Betty holds her champagne glass out to Gigi. "I'm getting too old not to say what I'm feeling and thinking, baby. I don't know how much time I have left here with you kids to point you in the right direction."

"You're not going anywhere anytime soon, auntie. I forbid it," Gigi says, filling Betty's glass to the top.

"If it were only that simple, kiddo," Betty replies. "Now, let's toast my granddaughter and her new handsome devil."

Once Gigi's done filling the flutes, we lift them into the

air, and Betty clears her throat. "To eternal love that burns bright and long."

We clink our glasses together and then take a sip. The champagne's bitter and has never been my favorite thing to drink, but I do it to appease Betty.

"You made this old woman very happy tonight," Betty says, but she isn't looking at any one person. "There's nothing better than being surrounded by family."

I take in her words, hating that I'll never have this with my family. Sure, I have my mom and kids, but I can't imagine Thumper ever settling down. And even if he did, we don't like each other enough to be thankful for our time together. I wouldn't think our kids would be friends because we aren't. We are a fractured family, but that is my brother's choice by being a dipshit his entire life.

"How are your parents?" Betty asks as I slide my hand under the table and intertwine my fingers with Tate's.

She doesn't even look my way as their length tightens around mine. "I miss them," Tate says to Gigi.

"They're good. Busy as ever with the grandkids. I didn't think they'd be better grandparents than parents, but they've proven me wrong. They live and breathe for them. Dad works sometimes when he needs a break from retirement, which is getting to be more and more. I think he has a hard time realizing he's getting older."

"Oh, he knows, baby. He just doesn't like it. No one does," Betty explains.

From her lips to God's ears. Every single new pain is a reminder that my body is already starting to break down, and I hate every minute of it.

"But they're great, otherwise. Just as in love as they always were."

"Joey was such a little troublemaker. I still can't wrap my head around him with your mother. She's a good girl."

"Dad's the best, auntie," Gigi tells Betty.

Betty chuckles into her champagne flute. "He is, but when he was young...phew. The man was a hellion."

"Well, isn't that the Gallo way? Which one of your kids was the angel?"

Betty smirks. "Not a damn one of them. We have to marry the good ones so our blood doesn't become too corrupted. We're already hell on wheels."

"Where's everyone else?" Gigi asks, looking around the bar. "I was hoping to see the other cousins."

"They'll be around all week, and if they aren't, we're having a family dinner before you guys head back," Tate tells her cousin. "You're stuck with just us tonight."

"It's okay," she says, "I'm exhausted anyway. Traveling always sucks the life out of me, and tomorrow's going to be another long day."

"You don't have a client until two. I made sure not to book you too early."

"You're a smart cookie, Tate Gallo," Gigi replies, giving her cousin a big smile.

"You want to get out of this place?" Tate asks me. "You can walk me home."

"Yeah, princess. Let's go."

I'm not going to let a single evening go to waste while the girls are away at camp.

I lean over, placing my lips next to Tate's ear. "I guess I didn't fuck you good enough the last time if you didn't realize you are mine. We're going to fix that tonight."

Tate swallows as her eyes darken, and she turns her

head so her gaze meets mine. "Don't promise me a good time if you aren't going to deliver."

"Tomorrow, you're going to walk funny."

She smirks. "Bet."

"Bet."

CHAPTER 23
TATE

I LOST THE BET.

It was the only time in my life when I didn't mind being wrong.

Even my toes are sore today because they remained in a curled position for far too many minutes.

"I see Wylder outdid himself," Gigi says to me as soon as I walk inside Inked.

"I stubbed my toe."

My cousin looks me up and down and laughs. "Ride a horse last night after you stubbed your toe, too?"

I give her the middle finger, hobbling toward the front desk a little after one. "I feel like I did." I ease into my chair, feeling like I sat on a hot poker. "Damn," I whisper.

Gigi smirks, watching me like a hawk. "I remember those days. Great times."

"Doesn't feel so great," I mutter.

"I really like Wylder. The last one was so…"

"They know each other."

Gigi's eyebrows rise. "They do? How?"

"Wylder's brother is in the same MC as Rowdy."

Gigi gasps, slapping the desk with her flattened palms. "Get the fuck out of here. The same one that wanted you dead?"

"Yep."

"Fuuuuck," she hisses. "That's a clusterfuck."

"He and Wylder already had some tense words over me."

"Was he the one who ordered the hit?"

"No, but he didn't do anything to stop it."

"Well, duh. Once an order is given, no one can pull it back but the prez. I know that. Is he an asshole?"

"He wasn't before they tried to kill me. I always got along with him, but it's hard to let go of the memory when someone would've put a bullet in your head."

Gigi nods. "Girl, that's bananas. What are you going to do?"

I shrug. "They don't get along, so it's not like I have to be around him. Am I being an idiot?"

"About the brother?" she asks me.

"All of it," I say, dragging my hands down my face. "The brother. The fact that Wylder's more than a decade older than me. He's a single dad. There are so many things that should have me running for the hills, but I can't stop myself from wanting to be around him. One look, and he sucks me right in."

"Does he treat you like shit when no one's around?"

"Oh my God. No. He's amazing."

"Older single dads are hot, girl. Guys like Rowdy are a dime a dozen, but Wylder... He's like the holy grail. Mature, responsible, attentive, kind."

"A great fuck," I whisper, but loud enough for her to hear.

"We'll move that to the number one descriptor."

And as if he can hear us talking about him, my phone rings, his face popping up on the screen. It's the photo I snapped of him when he was undressing, and good God, it's just as hot as watching it in real life.

"Lord," Gigi mumbles. "Good job, girl."

"Thanks," I say, giving her a smile as I pick up my phone and answer. "Hey, baby."

"Hey, princess. I'm going to be gone all day. I got a call from the camp, and Hazel fell. They think she broke her collarbone, and she's at the hospital now. I'm going to go get her and bring her home."

My stomach drops, thinking of little Hazel hurt and alone.

"Oh my goodness. That's horrible. She has to be so scared."

"Maddy's with her. She said Hazel's taking it surprisingly well. The summer of freedom may be over, and we didn't really get a chance to start."

"It's okay, Daddy."

"I don't know how I feel about that word coming out of your mouth."

"Sorry," I say, cringing. I've never been with a real daddy before, and what used to be a sexy little nickname doesn't hit the same when he's an actual father. "Want me to come?"

"I know you have clients today. Stay here. I'll get her and bring her home. Swing by after work if you want. If you get there before me, the key's under the mat."

He and I are going to have to have a conversation

about safety. Leaving a key under the mat is a no-no. I thought everyone in the world knew that, but obviously, when you're a man, you don't put that much thought into your safety, or you figure it'll never happen to you.

"I want. Give her a kiss from me."

"Will do, princess. Later."

"Later," I tell him as he hangs up.

"What's wrong?"

"Hazel, the youngest, fell at camp, and they think she broke something."

"Damn," she mumbles. "Bye-bye, summer of fun."

"It's okay. We had a few nights, and I love the girls. They remind me so much of myself when I was younger. I just hope she's okay. I know I'd be scared to be hurt without my dad around."

"I'm such a sucker for my dad. He was the only one who could keep me calm when things were going to shit around me."

"Me too," I breathe, trying to ease my stomach. "I'm going to cancel my last client so I can be free when they get back."

"What's up with the mom?"

"Well, she's…" I spend the rest of the hour explaining everything that happened with Katie. I go into every gory detail I know from my family and from Wylder himself. When I finish, Gigi looks dumb struck.

"What in the actual fuck? Who does that shit to their own kids?" is her immediate response.

"A psycho."

She nods quickly. "I want to track her ass down and put my fist right into her face."

"That's my plan if I ever lay eyes on her. And the girls

—" I shake my head, trying to tamp down my anger "—are the best and cutest things you've ever seen. They're sweet, smart, and a little mischievous. If I could design two little girls for myself, they would be it."

"If shit works out between you two, they may be just that. She's out of the picture, so you'd be their mom. Could you handle that?"

"I think so," I tell her truthfully. "I'm sure it wouldn't be easy, but I'd give them all the love I have to give."

"Kids are easy. Mouthy as fuck sometimes and full of attitude, but food, water, love, candy, and voilà, happy buggers."

"Is it really that easy?" I ask her.

"No." She chuckles. "But it's the lie I tell myself. I just want them to grow up and be happy. I don't want to be the reason they're in therapy as adults."

I can't stop the laughter that bursts from my lips.

"What are you two laughing about?" Pike asks as he walks into the shop, his shirt lifted a bit as he scratches his stomach. His hair is wild as hell like he rolled out of bed and stalked into the room. I can see why my cousin fell hard for the guy. He is mint.

"Not wanting to traumatize our kids so they end up in therapy."

"You're the best mom," he tells her as he leans over, kissing the top of her head.

She casts her gaze at him, smiling with so much love it makes my heart ache. "You're a good liar, baby."

I've always wanted a love like theirs, and for the first time in my life, I feel like I'm the closest I've ever been. I can picture Wylder and me ten years from now, and it would be this. The girls would be grown and maybe out of the house, living a crazy life at a college in a warm and sunny location.

"There's something different about you today," Pike tells me as his eyes search my face.

"The girl got dicked down properly," Gigi tells him.

I want to climb under the desk and die. Who says shit like that? My cousin. And the only person worse than her is another one of my cousins, Tamara. The mouths on those two are ridiculous.

"Well, okay then. That'll do it," he says with a slight chuckle as he walks to the back of the shop.

I smack my cousin on the shoulder, but not with any anger or hatred. "Stop telling people about my sex life."

She brushes me off like I am a tiny gnat bumping into her. "He's not people. He's my husband, and the man knows what a proper dick down means. It's how he made me fall in love with him."

"Some things are meant to be private," I tell her, pushing away from the desk, ready to start the day.

"Then don't walk like you still have his cock lodged in your vagina. It's hard to ignore the telltale signs of a great dicking, baby girl."

I give her the middle finger again, the conversation dying as soon as a customer walks in the door.

Thankfully, he's there for Gigi, and his wife is getting inked by Pike. I have fifteen more minutes to get my shit together and figure out a way to walk like a normal human being.

———

The sun has set by the time I pull in front of Wylder's house. The lights are on, but the Scout isn't there. I hope the truck didn't take a shit on the way home again. That would suck.

Maybe he ran out so fast after the phone call, he forgot to turn off the lights. I do things like that all the time when I'm in a panic and moving faster than my mind.

Wylder last texted me two hours ago, letting me know they were within a few hours, so I figured he'd be here by now.

When I make it to the front door, it's cracked open, and music is coming from the back of the house where the kitchen is.

"Hello," I call out as I push open the door and look around, seeing and hearing no one. "Anyone here?" I wait a moment for a reply before stepping inside.

I push the door closed behind me, not bothering to lock it. If they're not here, they will be any minute.

"Hello," I call out again when I hear the scraping of something in the kitchen.

This is how so many horror films I've watched start out before one of the boneheaded characters is offed by a psychotic murderer. I always laugh and think of how stupid they were for falling for it, but here I am, doing the same shit.

I grab a metal candleholder off the coffee table and tiptoe toward the back of the house. If someone is here, I'm not going to be empty-handed.

And when I round the corner, I see something I haven't prepared myself for.

A woman stands dead center in the kitchen, apron on, mixing something up in a giant bowl. She screams when she sees me, nearly jumping out of her skin. "Who are you?" she asks, pointing the giant wooden spoon at me. "Get out of here before I call the cops."

I stare at her, dumbfounded. "This isn't your house. Who the fuck are you?"

She moves around the small island, dropping the spoon, and grabs the knife she must've left there when prepping whatever the hell she's making in a kitchen that isn't hers. "This *is* my house."

"Listen, lady. I don't know where you think you are, but this isn't your home," I tell her as I take steps backward, trying to make my way to the door to run. "This is Wylder's house."

She sneers at me, matching me step for step. "I know. He's my husband," she says, turning up her nose.

I blink in confusion. "Katie?" I ask, my voice low and unsteady.

"Yes, I'm Wylder's wife."

"Ex," I say, but my feet don't stop moving.

If she didn't have a knife in her hand, I'd be a little more challenging, but I'm not about to go toe-to-toe with a knife-wielding nutjob.

"You gave up that title when you married someone else." I don't know why I'm engaging with her. I have a feeling it doesn't matter what I say; she has her own loony version of the story.

"I'm back now. Who are you?" she asks, looking like she stepped out of that Hitchcock movie where the person is stabbed in the shower.

"You're back?"

She nods. "I am. This is my home. My husband. My kids."

"Um, you may want to talk to Wylder about that."

She lunges forward, the knife nicking my arm. I lurch back in pain, pulling my arm against my chest as I scramble backward faster than before. But before I can get too far, the front door bursts open.

"What in the actual fuck," the loud, booming voice says as my back collides with their front. "Katie, you fucking crazy bitch."

But then, I'm pushed to the side as Thumper, not Wylder, hurls himself at Katie, grabbing the knife right out of her hand. He doesn't hesitate a single moment before putting himself in harm's way to disarm Katie and rescue me from a situation that could've very easily ended another way.

"I knew you were fucked up in the head, but I never would've pegged you for a knife-wielding killer. Jesus fuck," he hisses as Katie stares at him, her mouth almost foaming around the corners.

"She stole my family!" Katie screams straight into Thumper's face.

I hold my arm, watching the entire show taking place right in front of me. Who would've ever thought Thumper would've saved me? Weird shit happens all the time, and this is a testament to that.

Before Thumper can do anything else, Katie lunges at him, jumping into the air like she's part of the circus. Before she's on top of him, he reaches his arm out, clocking her right in the face.

The furniture rattles as Katie hits the floor, knocked out cold from Thumper's fist.

"Holy fuck," I whisper.

She had that one coming. I don't like when men lay

hands on a woman, but Katie deserved that. I'm not sure there would have been anything else that could have stopped her from continuing the assault on him—or me, for that matter.

"I didn't want to do that," he says to me, like I'm judging him for doing what was necessary.

"I think she lost her mind. She wasn't going to stop otherwise."

"Where the fuck is Wylder?"

"Hazel broke something, so he had to go pick her up at camp. They'll be back any minute."

"Damn it," he seethes, dropping the knife on the small side table near the couch. "I'm getting her out of here before the girls come home and see their mom laid out."

"Where are you taking her?"

"The compound."

"The compound?" My eyebrows rise. Nothing good happens there, but I suppose she doesn't deserve a stay at the Ritz.

"I know a doc. I'll see if he can do a psych commit on her for a few days to see what the hell is going on. I'd hate to call the cops, because well…"

"Criminal aspect seems to get in the way sometimes, huh?"

Thumper chuckles as he bends down, grabbing Katie's limp body like she's a sack of potatoes. "Something like that. You want her arrested?"

I shake my head. "No. The girls don't need to hear about this."

His gaze dips to my arm. "Bandage that up before they get back. Wash it first to clean it and then stop that bleeding. You don't want that shit getting infected."

"Okay," I tell him, still in shock over everything that happened.

Thumper stalks across the living room, Katie hanging from his shoulders with her arms swaying with each step.

"I was never here. She was never here. Got me?"

"Got you," I say as he disappears into the night, closing the door behind him.

CHAPTER 24
WYLDER

"YOU COULD'VE STAYED AT CAMP," I say to Maddy as we pull up in front of the house right behind Tate's car. "I can drive you back tomorrow."

She shakes her head, pulling at her bottom lip. "I had enough wilderness for this summer, and you need someone to watch Hazel while you work since we're back."

I hate that she's right. If Hazel's home, I do need Maddy around at least for a few more years. Although Hazel's sometimes more mature than her sister, I still wouldn't feel right with leaving her for any amount of time.

"I'm sorry." I try to pull up a smile at her in the rearview mirror.

"Don't be. I'm only sorry Hazel broke her arm. The bugs and spiders were ridiculous there."

Thankfully, it wasn't her collarbone. It was a clean break of her arm and didn't require surgery. She is still going to have a miserable hot summer with the bulky cast the hospital put on her.

"So, no camp next year?" I ask Maddy, staring down at Hazel, who's already fiddling with her cast.

"No. We'll go back. Maybe it won't be as bad next year."

"She said the boys were hot," Hazel adds to the conversation, making me not like camp for her next year anymore.

"Zip it, Hazel," Maddy says as she pushes open the truck door.

"Be nice to your sister," I tell her, which earns me an eye roll.

Ah. My girls are back.

"Sheesh," Hazel says as she reaches for the door with her good arm, "you'd think she's the one who broke her arm. Crabby."

I smile at my girl, loving her to bits and hating that she broke her arm when I wasn't around to make her feel safe. "It happens."

Hazel stops before she climbs out and whispers, "PMS."

I chuckle to myself as I get out of the truck, rounding the front before Hazel has a chance to hop down. I help her out of the truck, earning myself a light kiss to the cheek. "Thanks, Daddy."

"Welcome, baby."

She holds my hand as we walk up to the front door, seeing Tate moving around the living room at a frantic pace. As soon as Maddy opens the door, Tate plops down on the couch, pretending she was relaxing.

"Hey, you," Tate says, breathing heavily. "I've missed you two."

Maddy runs to Tate, throwing herself against her on the couch. "It was soooo awful," she whines.

Tate wraps her arms around Maddy and laughs. "I'm sure it wasn't that bad."

Maddy pulls away and stares at Tate. "Worse than you could ever imagine."

"Hey," Hazel says, drawing Tate's attention away from Maddy. "I'm the one who's hurt here."

Tate chuckles as Maddy groans and climbs to the other side of the couch, making a spot for Hazel. Not a moment later, Hazel crashes into Tate, nearly knocking her in the jaw with her giant cast.

"Oh my goodness," Tate says, giving Hazel a bear hug. "Are you okay, baby?"

"It hurt," Hazel tells her, eating up the attention.

The girl was a trooper, though. I've broken shit and it hurts like a motherfucker, but this kid acted like it wasn't nearly as painful as I knew it had to be.

"What on earth happened?" Tate asks her as she settles Hazel in her lap.

I collapse into the chair next to the couch, watching my three girls. This is how life should be. They need a tender touch sometimes, and no matter how hard I try, I can't always be that for them. There's nothing like the tenderness of a female, and Tate gives it to them, no matter that she didn't birth the girls herself.

"I was running through the woods, and I don't know..." Hazel shrugs. "The next thing I knew, I was on the ground, skidding across the grass, and in so much pain."

Tate cups Hazel's face and kisses her cheek gently. "Poor baby."

"I know," Hazel says with a pout. "I think I need ice cream to make me feel better or one of your Shirley Temples."

"We have ice cream in the freezer," I tell her.

Tate glances over at Maddy. "I need to talk to your dad for a minute. Can you get her the ice cream?"

This isn't good. No good conversation starts with needing to speak away from the kids. Something happened, and I have a feeling I'm not going to be happy about it.

"We can grab their stuff out of the truck."

"Fine," Maddy says, like we're somehow putting her out. "Do you two want any?"

"No," I reply as Tate shakes her head in response.

"We won't be long," Tate tells her as Hazel climbs off Tate's lap and makes a beeline for the kitchen.

We stay where we are until the girls are out of the room. "What's wrong?" I ask.

She ticks her head toward the door. "Out there."

I push myself up and head toward the door, wanting to know what happened. Tate hadn't acted any differently since we walked through the door. Whatever it is, she has been good at masking that something is wrong.

As soon as we're outside, she throws herself into my arms. "Oh my God. It was so horrible," she cries, curling her fingers into my T-shirt.

I grab her arms and hold her. "What happened?"

"K-katie," she stammers.

My entire body goes rigid. "Katie what?" I ask, looking around and seeing no one but us outside.

Tate tips her head back, staring up at me with tears swimming in her eyes. "She was here."

My heart stutters in my chest, and all the air in my lungs vanishes. "She what?"

Tate pulls back a little, keeping her hands balled in my shirt. "I got here, and the door was cracked open and all the lights were on."

A sudden sense of dread comes over me. "Is she here still?"

"No. Thumper took her."

"What?" I ask through gritted teeth.

"She went bananas. When I walked in, she told me she was your wife and came after me with a knife."

The amount of rage coursing through my system is enough to make me almost levitate off the ground. "She what?" I ask again, because I can't believe what she's telling me. "Are you hurt?"

Tate pulls up the sleeve of her sweatshirt, showing me a poorly bandaged wound that has blood seeping out. "Just a small nick."

I grab her arm, inspecting the dressing. "A nick? That's more than a nick, princess. Where's Katie now? And how the hell does my brother fit into the night?"

"I don't know. He just showed up out of nowhere and took the knife from her. She wasn't happy about that and lunged at Thumper, and he laid her out. I don't mean he knocked her down—I mean he knocked her clean out. He left with her slung over his shoulder and told me to clean my wound."

This is a lot to process in a short amount of time. My bitch of an ex-wife was here, she attacked my girl, and could've very easily hurt the kids. Thank God they were at camp and not at the house when Katie decided she wanted back into our life.

"Thumper saved me. The night could've ended very differently."

"Huh," I mutter, surprised as hell.

"I know, right?

"We need to change that and clean it properly," I tell her, still holding her arm.

"I scrubbed it with soap. It's good."

"Then you need a new dressing."

"It's fine," she tells me again.

"No, princess. It's not. You're going to start dripping blood soon, and the girls will have questions. I'm going to dress it for you when we go inside."

"Okay," she breathes, collapsing against my chest again. "I was so scared, Wylder. What if the girls had been here when Katie did that?"

"I don't even want to imagine it."

"She's fucking crazy. Like, totally whacked out of her mind."

"Did Thumper say where he was taking her?"

"He said no cops and that he was taking her to the compound to see if their doc could put her on a psych hold to get evaluated."

Katie's lucky she's in my brother's hands and not mine. She deserves to be locked up and not just for a little while.

"He said it would be too traumatic for the girls if the cops got involved."

"Fuck," I hiss, hating that he is right.

"I thought he was right, so I cleaned up the house and myself and did my best to pretend nothing happened."

"Baby, you should get an award for tonight. I wouldn't have had a clue if you hadn't told me."

She finally smiles, but it's not as big and bright as usual. "I'm just really lucky that your brother decided to stop by when he did, or I don't know if I'd be breathing right now."

The door opens, and Hazel pops her little head out. "Tate, Maddy made you a sundae," she says, all the pain from earlier forgotten.

Tate gives me wide eyes and takes a deep breath like she's sliding into a different role before she turns toward Hazel. "Sounds delicious," she says to her. "I'll be right in."

Hazel smiles, her eyes moving between Tate and me. "You sure you don't want one, Daddy?"

"I'm good, baby," I tell her because I have other shit to do than enjoy ice cream with my girls because my ex-wife had to fuck shit up again.

"Okay, but you're missing out," she says before she closes the door, leaving us to finish our conversation.

Tate leans into me again, wrapping her arms around my middle as she does. "I better go inside before they get suspicious."

I bend my neck, pressing my lips to her hair. "I'm going to call Thumper and grab the bags."

"Don't be too long. I'm sure Maddy's already wondering what's going on."

"I'll make it quick," I tell her, knowing my elder daughter and her ability to figure out when shit is off.

Tate peers up at me, and I grab her face between my palms, kissing her gently. "I'm sorry," I whisper against her lips.

"It's not your fault."

"Yes, it is," I tell her because I brought Katie into my world...into her world.

"I'm fine, Wylder. I've had worse injuries from riding my bike."

Her words don't make the sting deep in my chest hurt any less.

"When you talk to Thumper, tell him thank you."

"I will, princess," I tell her as she pulls away and heads toward the front door.

I wait until she's inside and there's no chance of the girls walking out on my conversation to call my brother and find out what the hell is going on.

"Yo," Thumper says. "Guess you talked to Tate?"

"Yep. Where is she?"

"Tied up and passed out. The doc will be here soon, and then she'll be off to the hospital for a few days."

This isn't the best way to handle the situation, but right now, I have no other options. Katie needs help. Although she was always a massive bitch, the woman I knew would've never come after someone with a knife and then attacked a man more than twice her size.

"How badly is she hurt?" I ask him as I walk toward the truck to get farther out of earshot.

"I think I broke her nose, but other than that, she's fine. It's crooked as fuck, and I'm sure by tomorrow she'll have two massive black eyes."

"I can't believe you knocked her out, Thump."

"Wylder, she came at me. I've never seen anything like it. It was like she lost her ever-loving mind. It was the only thing I could do. It was a knee-jerk reaction. I'd never hit a woman, but she was possessed. I didn't even mean to do it. My arm just swung, and my fist connected with the target."

"Thank fuck you were here."

"I talked to sis and had a heart-to-heart about you and what an asshole I am. She told me if I didn't talk to you and be nice to Tate, she'd never speak to me again. So, I decided to come over and try to make peace."

"Ivy's always so bossy." Our sister isn't shy or demure. She grew up with three rough and completely asshole brothers. She is ruthless, but she had to be to survive around us. "She wouldn't have cut ties with you, though."

"You think so? I think she would've without a second thought. She said she was done with my shit."

I chuckle, imagining her laying into him. "I think we're all done with your shit."

"Why am I such an asshole?"

"That's a question you have to ask yourself. We're not your enemy, but you treat us like we are sometimes."

"Anyway, we'll get into my fucked-up shit another time. I'm just glad Ivy called and I decided to take a drive. The entire situation would've gone to shit if I hadn't shown up when I did. A few minutes would've meant the end of Tate."

"I wish I could come to the compound, but I can't leave the kids."

"I got this shit handled. How's my Hazelbug?"

"She's okay right now, but her arm's going to hurt like a bitch later."

"Can I drop by tomorrow and see her after I get Katie all sorted?"

"Of course."

"Thanks. Poor kid."

"Hey," I say, grabbing the last bag from the back. "Tate wanted me to tell you thank you."

"No problem. I'm glad I could help."

"And I wanted to say thank you too, brother."

"It's what I should've always been doing. Looking out for you and yours, Wyld. I'm sorry I've been a shithead your entire life."

"I'm sure you were before I was born, too," I tell him, and he bursts into deep, loud laughter.

"Later," he tells me.

I don't get a chance to say goodbye before he disconnects the call.

I stand outside on the street, watching Tate, Maddy, and Hazel in the living room. They're talking as they shovel ice cream into their mouths, looking so damn happy.

This is what life's all about, and I almost lost it in the blink of an eye.

CHAPTER 25
TATE

"YOU LOOK LIKE SHIT TODAY," Gigi says as she sits down next to me at the front desk of Inked.

"I feel like shit today."

"What happened? Is Hazel okay?"

I give her a sorrowful smile. "She's good, but something happened before they got home last night, and it has me reeling."

"What'd Wylder do?"

I shake my head. "It was his ex."

Her eyebrows crinkle together. "Doesn't she live out of state?"

"Yep," I snap before sighing. "I walked into Wylder's last night before they got back, but the house wasn't empty."

Her eyes widen. "Oh shit."

"It gets worse."

"How in the hell does it get worse?"

I push back the arm of my sweatshirt, showing her the bandage on my arm. "She had a knife."

Gigi jerks her head back as her eyes grow to be as big as I've ever seen them. "She fucking stabbed you?"

"She nicked me."

"Nicked you?"

"It's not that bad. Wylder bandaged it for me."

"Oh goodness. Were the girls hysterical?"

"They weren't there, and everything was cleaned up before they got back."

She leans in close, dropping her voice as she gazes around to see who is listening in on our conversation. "Everything was cleaned up?"

"His brother showed up at the perfect time and took her."

"Took her where?"

"The compound."

"For real?"

"For real, but he said their doctor was going to have her put on a psych hold."

She exhales. "Man, I thought they..." She runs her finger across her neck.

"I don't think so. As far as I know, she's alive and breathing," I say with a shrug, because I'm only going on Thumper's word.

"Clubs don't fuck around, and from what I know about that one, death is always on the table."

"Wylder is heading over there as we speak to see what's what."

"The man has to be beside himself," she replies.

"He's livid."

"Life is way livelier up here than back home."

"That's not a good thing," I tell her as I grab a scrap

piece of paper off the desk and crumple it into a ball. "I could use a little quiet."

She snorts so loud, she covers her mouth to stifle the noise. "Nah, it's totally overrated. I mean, I could do without the knives, but a little drama always keeps the blood pumping."

"What keeps the blood pumping?" Pike asks as he walks into the front, followed by his client.

"Nothing," I mumble because the last thing I want to do is talk about my life drama in front of a customer. I'm used to listening to their stories, but they sure as hell don't need to hear mine.

"We'll tell you later. Something that happened last night to Tate," Gigi tells her husband.

I grab my phone, busying myself while Pike cashes out his client. So far, their guest spot at Inked has been a huge success. Gigi never doubted that having the Florida crew come north to do work would be big business. Social media makes it possible to get the word out and expand their client and fan base.

The original Florida location became popular during her parents' heyday with magazine spotlights and only grew as social media came on the scene. With daily posts, live videos, and international merch, everyone in the tattoo community learned about Inked and their artists.

As soon as I open my texting app, three dots appear. It's like we're cosmically connected sometimes.

Wylder: She's locked up for a few days. Thumper has some pull with a judge and may be able to extend it to ninety.

I stare at the message, blinking rapidly. Ninety fucking days is a long-ass time. It's almost scary to think that with a few phone calls, anyone with enough connections can have someone put away without their consent. Scary as fuck.

Me: That's good...I guess.

Wylder: I'll call her husband and let him know where she is.

Me: That sounds like a fun conversation.

Wylder: It's not one I want to have.

My cousin Lulu strolls through the door, looking like she's about to do a photo shoot for a fashion magazine. "Cousin," she coos, sliding her sunglasses on top of her head, "I was walking by and had to say hi."

Gigi stands from her chair and rounds the desk. "You never have an uggo day," Gigi tells her as they kiss on both cheeks.

"I have an early dinner date with some potential investors. It's not how I want to spend my evening, but I'm going to make the best of it," Lulu explains.

Lulu's trying to get a start-up off the ground, but I don't know much about it. She's been very hush-hush about most of the details because she's scared she won't get enough investors for it to become a real, tangible thing. She's never liked to fail at anything, and I have a feeling this will be no different. She and the company will be a smashing success.

"Where are you going at this hour dressed like that?" I point to her fancy outfit, giving it a once-over with a wave of my finger.

"Some place over on Wabash near the old Marshall Field's. He insisted I come toward downtown to meet him."

"There are some amazing new food spots down there, though."

"Isn't this downtown?" Gigi asks, staring at us like we have two heads.

"We're not downtown. We're in a neighborhood."

"But it's all Chicago?" she asks, needing clarification.

"Yes."

"Chicagoans are weird."

"Not going argue that point," I tell her.

Lulu looks every bit like her mom, Delilah. She's my cousin by marriage and not blood, but it doesn't make us love each other any less. We grew up together, causing trouble and sharing secrets we wouldn't share with anyone else in the world.

"You know what I want," Gigi says, changing the course of the conversation. "I want to go to Chinatown and eat before I leave. I want all the Chinese food I can fit in here." She rubs her stomach and smiles. "I can already taste it."

"We can head to Chinatown tonight if we're done early enough," I tell her.

She fist-pumps the air and does a small little hip dance.

"See, that's not considered downtown. You said China-town because it's a neighborhood," I explain.

"Whatever. Just take me there," she begs.

"Okay, okay."

"I'm coming," Lulu adds. "After my meeting, I'll run home and change into something more comfortable and normal. Text me when you guys know if you're going and when to meet you there. I haven't been there in a while, and I want to spend more time with my cousins. I've been working too much lately."

"We deserve a girls' night. Let the boys do whatever boys do," I say.

"Scratch their balls and watch sports," Gigi adds, making us all giggle.

"Girls' night at the Evergreen."

"Sounds like heaven," Lulu breathes as she pushes her sunglasses back on her nose. "I'm off. Wish me luck. I'm asking for a million today."

I nearly choke on my own spit as she strides toward the door with her head held high and an air about her that says money. "Good luck," I call out as she walks outside. "Sheesh. Only a million?"

Gigi laughs as she shakes her head. "I wouldn't even know where to begin to do that."

"Lulu has a way with people, especially men. They follow behind her with their tongues hanging out, salivating."

"She's stunning."

"She is—and smart, too. But don't think she's always sweet. She'll kick any man in the balls and clock him right in the jaw if he gets too handsy. I've seen her do it. She may be small, but she's mighty."

"Our daddies all taught us well," Gigi says, and I nod because they've each spent countless hours showing us how to protect ourselves from any type of threat.

"Did I hear Chinese?" Pike asks from across the shop.

"Girls' night," Gigi calls out.

"Damn," he barks. "I want some."

"I'll bring you some back."

"Fine," he groans.

"Men." She shakes her head. "He can hang out at the bar until I get back."

"I'm sure they'll be happy to have him visit," I tell her. "He can watch the game."

"What game?" she asks me.

I shrug. "Fuck if I know, but I'm sure there is one."

She slaps my shoulder as she stands. "You're nuts."

"I know." I smile up at her. "But, like, you're not normal either."

"Normal is overrated," she says as she leaves the room and heads back toward her husband.

My phone rings as if Wylder has ESP. "Hey," he says as soon as I answer.

"Everything okay?" I ask him, panic suddenly climbing up my insides.

"Yeah. I just talked to Katie's husband."

"Oh boy," I whisper.

Wylder blows out a long, loud breath. "He told her he wanted a divorce last week, and she lost it on him. He hadn't seen her in a few days and wasn't sure where she was. I informed him about what happened and where she is. He said to do whatever we wanted, he was washing his hands of her."

I gasp, shocked even though I shouldn't be. I guess he finally realized what a selfish witch she was, too. "Really?"

"I guess she destroyed the house and took a baseball bat to his car. He called the cops on her too, but she had already disappeared by the time they came to take the report."

"Well, damn," I mutter. "So, what are you going to do?"

"We'll see what the doctor has to say, but it sounded like her husband wants her to do the ninety days if the judge approves it."

"Of course he does." Who wants to deal with someone clearly having an episode of some sort? No one wants her around, and that's all because of her actions and the decisions she's made in her life, which affect everyone else. "She's clearly going through something."

I can't feel sorry for Katie. She should be in jail. She deserves it after what she did last night. But I have no dog in this fight. Whatever her husband, Wylder, and Thumper want to do is fine with me. Does that make me a heartless bitch? I don't care.

"It's all of her own making," he says with no remorse. "Anyway, you coming over tonight?"

"We're having a girls' night and heading to Chinatown."

"Well, if you want to drop by afterward, send me a text, princess."

"You miss me?" I ask, teasing him.

"Always. And I know the girls would like to see you too."

"Way to guilt me, handsome. You know I'm a sucker for those two."

"You like them more than me, don't you?" he asks.

I smile to myself. "Maybe," I lie.

"I'll take whatever I can get."

"Maybe I'll see you later. Give the girls a hug from me."

"Will do, princess. Have fun."

"Later, Wylder."

"Later," he replies before I hit *end*.

"You better go to that man's house afterward," Gigi tells me as she walks back into the front, waiting for her next client. "You both need each other after what happened last night."

"We'll see what the night brings."

"It's going to bring your ass to his place," she tells me as she plasters a giant smile on her face to greet the woman walking through the door.

"Welcome to Inked. I'm Gigi. Can I help you?"

And just like that, the conversation is over.

CHAPTER 26
WYLDER

"IT'S A PRETTY DAY," Ma says as we watch the girls play on the swing set I built last year.

"Can't beat the summertime," I say to her, kicking back in my chair with a glass of my mother's sun-brewed sweet tea.

"Where's Tate?" Ma asks.

"She went out with the girls last night so she's running behind."

"Hello." Shadow's voice carries through the backyard.

I turn, confused as to why he's here. "What the…"

"So, I may have invited your siblings over," Ma says, not looking me in the eye. "I thought it would be a nice way to spend the day. I heard you and Thumper made some headway in finally moving beyond your differences."

If she weren't my mother, I'd argue with her. Our idea of differences is not the same. We don't disagree on the definition of love or the color of the sky. Thumper has spent his entire life making mine miserable. Shadow is better, but not by much. He's never set out to do bad to me, but he isn't the kind of brother I can always depend on. He is more worried about his own cock than his family.

"I brought wine," Ivy says as her dirty-blond ponytail sways with each step.

Close behind her, carrying a bag, is Thumper. And for the first time in as long as I can remember, a snarl doesn't form on my lips at the very sight of him.

"I brought gifts," he says, raising the brown bag high in the air to get the girls' attention, "for my favorite nieces."

Maddox and Hazel run from the swings and go barreling in his direction. "Uncle Thumper," they call in unison as they almost collide with him.

"What am I? Chopped liver?" Shadow asks them, pretending to be upset. But the man likes kids as much as he likes cops.

"You're annoying," Ivy tells him as she makes her way to the stone patio where we are sitting. "And a dumbass."

"Ivy," Ma chides her like Shadow hasn't said worse things to her over the years. "Be nice to your brothers."

Ma always wants us to be nice and get along, but it's never been in the cards. When half of the gang is made up of complete and utter assholes, it's hard to get that kumbaya bullshit other families have.

Ivy stops dead. "When Shadow and Thumper decide to stop being assholes, I'll be nice to them, Ma. Until then, they're getting what they're giving."

"Come on, sis. I'm nice," Shadow tells her as he brushes by her and knocks her in the shoulder.

"Shadow," Ma warns.

Ivy isn't even fazed by Shadow's attempt to knock her off-kilter. "Where's your woman, Wylder?"

"She's on her way. Although now, I'm regretting inviting her over," I say, looking between my brothers.

"I have no issue with Tate," Shadow says. "The past is the past."

"Easy for you to say since your life wasn't on the line," I remind him.

"My life's on the line every day with the club." He grabs a beer from the six-pack he had tucked under his arm when he strolled into the backyard. "That's life."

"It's not life for most people," Ma says, shaking her head at his answer. "Tate's a good girl."

"She's not hard on the eyes either," Shadow says in a low voice as he pulls the tab on the beer can.

"Daddy, Daddy," Hazel says, running across the yard with a pink stuffed animal in her hand. Her casted arm is swinging wildly with every step, and if she is in pain, she sure hasn't shown it. "Look what Uncle Thumper got me."

She shoves the stuffed animal in my face, making me pull back a little to focus on it. "It's so nice." It's both ugly as hell and the funniest thing I've ever seen, because whatever weird-ass animal it's supposed to be also has a cast on its arm.

"I love it," she says, squeezing it against her chest tightly. "It's just like me."

"Yeah, sweetheart. Just like you."

Out of the corner of my eye, I see Tate walk into the backyard and freeze. Her gaze moves around to my sister and then to my brothers before landing on me. I fully expect for her to turn around and haul ass right out of here. If I were in her shoes, it's what I would do.

Thumper's eyes land on Tate, and before I can get up, he starts walking in her direction. She lifts her hand at me, making me stay put.

If he is an asshole to her today, I'll throw him out on his ass and never let him back on my property again. I am not in the mood for his shit, and I am not going to put up with him disrespecting my girl.

Thumper rubs the back of his neck as he stops a few feet away from her. He talks first and she listens, staring up at him with no anger.

"What's that about?" Ivy asks as she sits down in the chair next to me, staring across the yard to where my eyes are pointed.

"I don't know," I lie.

"You must have a clue or else you would've had your ass over there already. You're a shit liar, Wylder," she tells me as she twists the top off the cheap wine she adores. It's garbage that doesn't even taste like wine and more like our favorite fruit punch as kids, but she loves the shit.

I don't reply. There's nothing I can say because she isn't wrong.

I curl my fingers around the armrest, doing my best to keep my ass in my seat but ready to jump up at any moment. But then I see Tate smile. A genuine smile. And it's directed at Thumper. I almost shit myself when she leans forward and wraps her arms around him.

"Huh," Ivy mutters. "The world must be coming to an end."

They pull apart after a few seconds, and Thumper has a smile on his face too.

"We're good," Tate calls out as they start walking in our direction.

"Weirdest shit I've ever seen," Ivy says before taking another sip of her wine.

I'm out of my seat a second later, heading toward Tate. I don't even look at Thumper because I need to know what was said first.

"You good?" I ask her, holding her face between my hands and staring deep into her eyes.

"He apologized for the past, and I thanked him for saving my life. We're square now."

"That simple?" I ask, finding it unbelievable.

"That simple. I can let shit go, especially when it involves me having the ability to still be standing here today. He could've let Katie kill me."

"Jesus," I whisper, thinking about that statement. He could've. I would've murdered him with my bare hands if he had, but he damn well could've let Katie kill her.

"It's time to bury the hatchet, Wylder. At least for me. I don't expect you to forgive him for all the shit in the past, but I'm going to for what he's done to me," Tate says.

"It's been a lifetime of shit," I reply.

"I know. But I love being with you and your girls. He's your brother, like him or not. He's going to be around, and I don't feel like constantly being at war with him every time we're together."

"Why do you have to be so smart?" I ask her, still holding her face. "I love being with you too, Tate, but if that means not having my brother in my life, so be it. He's made his choices."

"Again, he apologized. I'm good. We're good. But I'm thirsty and could really use a cold drink."

"Tate!" Maddy yells across the yard, waving her hands.

"Dad, let her go. We want to spend time with her too. Stop hogging Tate."

Tate smiles at me. "We better go, or else the teenager's going to lose her shit."

I sigh, resting my forehead against hers. "She's insufferable."

"You can have me all to yourself tonight."

"Promise?" I whisper.

Tate places her hands against my sides near the top of my jeans. "Promise."

"Tate. Tate. Tate," Hazel says, popping up next to us like she materialized out of thin air. "Look what Uncle Thumper brought me."

The moment we were having is over, but there's a promise of later. I'd hold on to that while trying to navigate the most dysfunctional impromptu family gathering in my own backyard.

Tate takes the toy from Hazel's hand, inspecting it as we walk toward the patio. "What is it?"

"I dunno. It's cute, though. Isn't it?" Hazel asks Tate as she reaches for her hand and curls her little fingers in Tate's palm.

"It's adorbs."

"We good?" Thumper asks me as we get closer. He looks hopeful, and there's a kindness in his gaze I'm not sure I've ever seen before.

"Yeah," I tell him. I can let the past lie until the next incident. I'll cross that bridge if and when I come to it.

"This is a good day," Ma says with the biggest smile. "All my kids and grandkids in the same place and no one's fighting."

"It's still early, Ma. Give us time," Shadow adds.

"Always have to open your mouth and ruin a good time, don't you, Shadow," Ivy says to my brother, but she doesn't bother looking at him when he speaks. "I'm sorry about him." She glances toward Tate as we sit. "He was dropped on his head too many times as an infant. I'm so happy to finally meet you."

"You too," Tate says, taking an empty glass when Ivy hands it to her.

"You're going to need wine."

"Wine is always a plus." Tate smiles at my sister, lifting the glass so Ivy can fill it.

"Uncle Thumper," Hazel says softly, giving him her pouty look. "Will you push me on the swing?"

Thumper gets up without a second thought, taking Hazel by the hand and leading her toward the swing set.

"She has him wrapped around her little finger," Tate says to me before she takes a sip of wine.

"Girls have a way of doing that to even the toughest guys," I tell her, and I'm totally talking about myself.

There isn't a thing I wouldn't do for any of the women in the backyard. I'd lay down my life to keep them safe. And for the first time in my entire life, I think my brothers would do the same, even for Tate.

CHAPTER 27
TATE

ONE YEAR Later

"Maddy, we're late!" I yell up the steps, glancing around the living room for my purse.

"One second!" she yells back.

Hazel rolls her eyes. "She's so slow."

I chuckle to myself, remembering a time when I was as slow as Maddy and probably annoyed the crap out of my younger brothers. But they'd never understand what being a teenage girl was like and how important appearance seemed to be during those years.

"We ready?" Wylder asks.

"Almost."

"Maddy's putting on her makeup," Hazel tells him with an eye roll.

His eyebrows wrinkle together in the adorable way they do when he's confused. "Makeup?"

"She says she has to look her best," Hazel says as if it should make complete sense to someone like Wylder. But she hasn't learned that boys, even older ones, don't think like women. They'll never understand the impossible standards we're held to and how we're judged on our outsides before anyone gets to know the real us.

"She's beautiful without all that garbage on her face."

"Wylder, leave her be. This time is important in a girl's life. She's finding herself. There's a lot of pressure on her, and I'm sure my family doesn't even realize we're not there yet. It's casual. You know that."

"What the hell does that mean?"

Hazel gasps. "That's a dollar, Dad."

Wylder mutters a curse word, and Hazel holds up two fingers.

"Fine," he says, reaching for his wallet and grabbing two ones from inside. "How's she finding herself in a bottle of mascara?"

"It's a tube," I reply.

"What's a tube?"

"It's a tube of mascara. Not a bottle."

He frowns at me, exasperated. It's an expression he wears more and more now, especially when it's something new with Maddy.

"Okay. A tube," he says, drawing out the word to be a brat.

"I'm done," Maddy says, barreling down the stairs. "We can go now."

"Finally," Wylder says, wound a little tighter than usual.

"Baby, it'll be okay," I reassure him, wanting him to have a good day.

"I want today to be perfect," he says.

"It will be." I smile at him.

"Who's ready to go eat?"

Hazel's the first one heading toward the door. "I'm having one of every dessert," she says before turning the knob.

"Of course you are," I tell her as I follow her out the door. "Who needs pasta when you can have cannoli?"

"Not me." She marches toward the car, looking older than she did the day before.

The girls are growing quickly. The features on their faces are changing rapidly. I don't think I'm ready for them to grow up. I can't imagine how my father felt seeing me change in every way right before his eyes.

"Do you think Nino will be there?" Maddy asks as we walk toward the bar on foot to enjoy the summer day.

It suddenly makes sense why she was so concerned about making sure her appearance was perfect. Maddy has a little crush on my cousin.

Of course, he is way too old for her, but that never stopped a teenage girl from trying.

"I think so. I'm not sure if he's done at school for the summer, though."

"Oh." Her shoulders sag a little like the air of possibility was instantly sucked out of her.

"Nino's nice," Hazel says as she stomps down the sidewalk in a new pair of sandals that are too big for her feet. "He makes funny faces."

Thank God Maddy and Hazel are so far apart in age. I'm not sure I could handle two girls in puberty and hitting their boy-crazy era at the same time.

I slide my hand in Wylder's, feeling the tension radiating off him. "What's wrong?"

"Nothing," he says, glancing at me for a moment. "I'm just hungry."

"Tate," Brax calls out, spotting us. "Wait up." He jogs across the busy street, weaving in and out of traffic.

"Hi," I say, lifting my free hand.

"Hey," Wylder greets him.

The girls give little waves to my brother before going back to their private conversation. Tomorrow, they leave for camp, trying it again and hoping for different results.

"Phew. I thought I was late, but at least I'm not walking in alone," Brax says, breathing heavily to try to catch his breath like he jogged here.

We're near Cheryl's house, and I expect her to be on the front porch, waiting for us. But she isn't. "Where's your Ma?" I ask Wylder as I stare at the now-empty chair she's always waiting in.

"Tate," Wylder says.

I turn my head, and he's not there. I look down, and he's on one knee with a small box in his hand.

My belly flips and my heart flutters. "What the..." I glance around. Brax has his phone pointed at us, and the girls are behind their dad with one hand on each of his shoulders.

"Tate—" Wylder clears his throat "—this is the very spot where I first laid eyes on you and everything in my world shifted. All the darkness that used to be there vanished. All the loneliness simply disappeared. My life changed in that moment. I found a woman who loves my girls like they were her own. Someone who could deal with my family, even my asshole brothers. A woman who loves me for me and expects nothing in return except love. A woman who makes me want to be a better man and give her the moon and the stars if I could."

"Wow, Daddy. Who knew you could say so many words at one time," Hazel says with a giggle.

I let out a bark of laughter as tears start to stream down my cheeks. Hazel always knows how to insert herself in a moment.

"Tate Gallo, will you marry me and officially be part of our family?" Wylder pulls back the lid to the box, exposing a small diamond ring.

"Oh my God," I breathe, my body humming and my heart pounding so fast, I think it could burst through my chest. The girls are smiling as big as I've ever seen, and Wylder's looking at me with so much love, I can't do anything else except say, "Yes."

Wylder scoops me into his arms, forgetting all about sliding the ring on my finger. I'm not even mad about that. There will be time for formalities afterward.

I press my lips to his as the girls celebrate behind him. "Yes, yes, yes," I murmur against his mouth, wrapping my arms around his neck and letting myself get lost in the moment.

It's then I realize he's shaking. It all clicks into place. His tenseness with a hint of grumpy. This is a big step for a man whose wife left him and his girls behind like they were nothing. Opening your heart to love again isn't a simple thing. But now, he's offering me forever with him and his girls.

"I love you," he breathes into my mouth.

"I love you too."

"Bleh." Hazel gags behind us. "Too much kissing."

"Stop it," Maddy says. "Let them have their moment. It's romantic."

We chuckle as we pull apart, and I slide down

Wylder's front until my shoes touch the cement. He stares at me like nothing else in the world matters.

In a whirlwind of a year, I've found the best boyfriend —now my fiancé—and two amazing girls who love me like I have been in their lives since they took their first breaths.

It's funny how fate works. If they hadn't wandered into the bar for a Shirley Temple, I probably wouldn't be standing here right now with my future in front of me.

He pulls out the ring with shaky hands before handing the empty box to Maddy. When he slides the metal over my finger, he says, "You're mine forever."

"I'm yours always," I whisper as Wylder lifts my hands to his mouth, kissing the ring he just placed there.

And no other words have ever felt so right.

Are you ready for more Gallos?

Brad Gallo's story is coming next...
visit *menofinked.com/want* to get your copy from your
favorite eBook retailers or order direct at chelleblissro-
mance.com

**Want to be the first to hear about the next Men of Inked
book or everything Chelle Bliss?** Join my newsletter by
visiting *menofinked.com/inked-news*

BECOME A MEMBER OF THE FAMILY...

Want a place to talk romance books, meet other bookworms, and all things Men of Inked? Join Chelle Bliss Books on Facebook to get sneak peeks, exclusive news, and special giveaways.

Want to be the first to hear about the next Men of Inked book or everything Chelle Bliss? Join my newsletter by visiting _menofinked.com/inked-news_ or scan the QR code below.

NEED MORE MEN OF INKED CHICAGO?

THE COMPLETE DIGITAL EBOOK COLLECTION

Have you read the Men of Inked Southside series? Visit
menofinked.com/southside to learn more and be prepared
for the Men of Inked Sinners, the next generation of the
Southside.

SIGNED PAPERBACKS ARE WAITING

Learn more at *chelleblissromance.com*

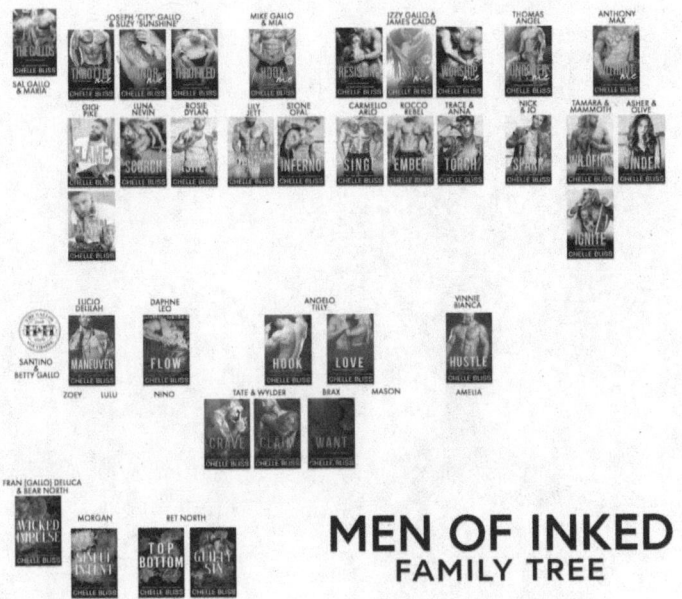

MEN OF INKED
FAMILY TREE

MENOFINKED.COM/BOOKS

Check out a bigger version at **_menofinked.com/gallo-family-tree_** or view the series reading order at **_menofinked.com/gallo-saga_**

ABOUT THE AUTHOR

I'm a full-time writer, time-waster extraordinaire, social media addict, coffee fiend, and ex-history teacher. *To learn more about my books, please visit menofinked.com.*

Want to stay up-to-date on the newest
Men of Inked release and more?
Join my newsletter at *menofinked.com/news*

Join over 10,000 readers on Facebook in Chelle Bliss Books private reader group and talk books and all things reading. Come be part of the family!

See the Gallo Family Tree

Where to Follow Me:

facebook.com/authorchellebliss1

instagram.com/authorchellebliss

bookbub.com/authors/chelle-bliss

goodreads.com/chellebliss

tiktok.com/@chelleblissauthor

amazon.com/author/chellebliss

pinterest.com/chellebliss10